Thomas Campion

The Lyric Poems of Thomas Campion

Thomas Campion

The Lyric Poems of Thomas Campion

ISBN/EAN: 9783744780131

Printed in Europe, USA, Canada, Australia, Japan

Cover: Foto ©Andreas Hilbeck / pixelio.de

More available books at **www.hansebooks.com**

CANTVS

IIII

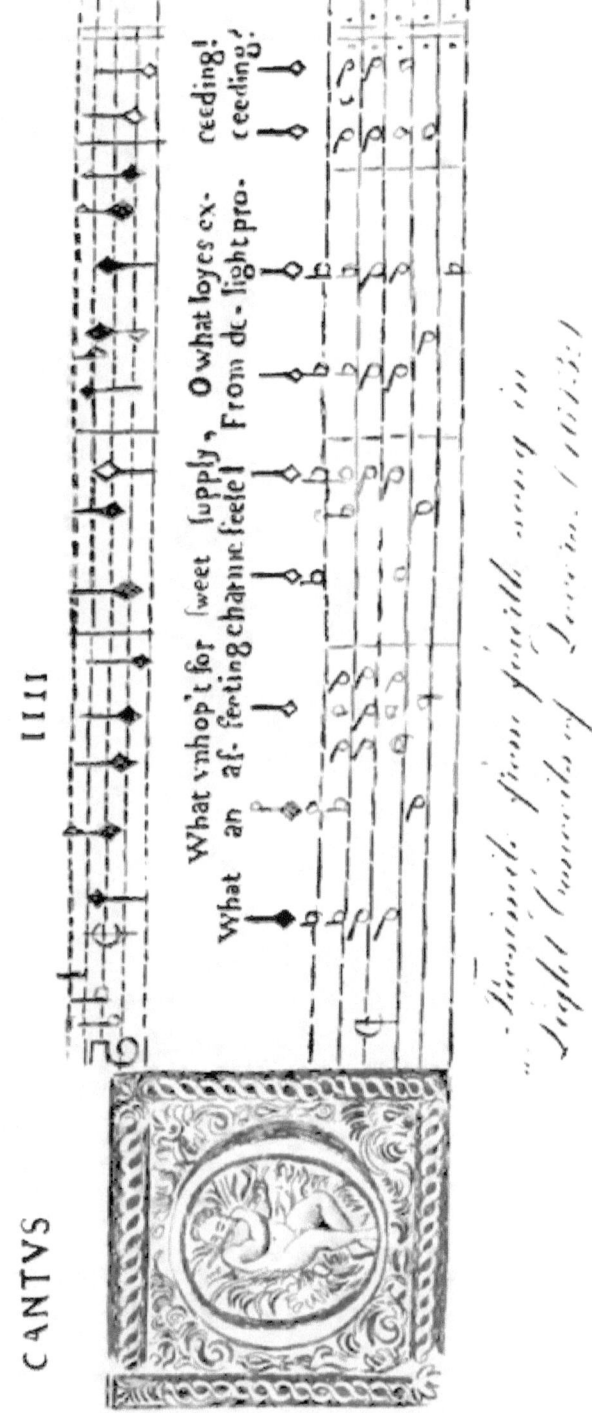

What vnhop't for sweet supply, O what loyes ex- ceeding!
What an af- fecting charme feele I From de- light pro- ceeding.

Facsimile from fourth song in
"Light Conceits of Louers" (1613?)

THE LYRIC
POEMS OF
THOMAS
CAMPION.

·EDITED·BY·ERNEST·
RHYS·

J.M.DENT·&C⁰·ALDINE·HOUSE
69·Gͭ·EASTERN·Sͭ LONDON·E.C.

CONTENTS

v

Contents.

Contents.

Contents.

Contents.

Contents.

Contents.

INTRODUCTION.

CAMPION was all but a lost poet when Mr
Bullen so fortunately came to his rescue six
years ago. His lyrics, with the exception of the
very few turned to account by modern musicians,
or given a place in the anthologies, lay buried
in the old music books in which they were first
published. And yet, if they had been left to the
famous obscurity of the British Museum, we had
lost perhaps the one poet who comes nearest to
fulfilling, in the genre and quality of his work,
the lyric canon in English poetry.

Campion did not write with a theoretic sense
only of the correspondence between music and
poetry. He wrote as a musician, and his songs
were really meant to be sung. His lyre was a
real instrument; that is to say, it was represented
by real instruments—the lute and the viol, sometimes the orpharion. His lyrics are as perfect
an instance, indeed, as we are likely to find, if
we keep to the stricter limits of the art, besides
having all the natural warmth of word, the
charm and inspiration, without which the mere
art avails nothing.

Of the author himself we still know too little.
That he was born midway in the sixteenth
century; that he seems to have gone to Cam-
bridge, with the idea of studying for the Bar,
and was presently admitted a member of Gray's

Introduction.

Inn,—in 1586? that he gave up the law for medicine, took his M.D., and became a practising physician; and that he contrived to practise, too, as a musician and poet throughout his life: there is in outline all we know. He died in February 1619-20. On the first of March in that year, the entry, "Thomas Campion, Doctor of Physicke, was buried," is made in the register of St Dunstan's-in-the-West, Fleet Street.

His first book, which serves to explain much about him that would else be left dark, and which may explain something too of the Latin ring in his English verse, was his *Poema* of 1595, a book of Latin epigrams. No copy of this edition has been discovered; but the Epigrams were issued in a later and much amplified collection in the year 1619, the year of his death, so that his first book was in a sense his last.

From it we learn more of the man, his personal effect, temper and way of life, friends, enemies, quarrels, and the rest, than we should else have ever known. Throughout his career, with its vicissitudes of law and medicine, it is clear he moved in the leisured and courtly circles that his particular genius might seem to demand. His troubles seem to have been slight; enough for maturing the man, not enough for embittering him. His malice, peeping slyly out in his quips at Barnabe Barnes and Nicholas Breton, or in his references to more than one lady of his acquaintance, works in an idle vein, showing that his cause of complaint against men and things was at no time very serious. He strikes one as

Introduction.

a quite excellent example of that type of cul-
tured physician which we have all known; whose
art of healing only serves as an agreeable basis
for the liberal arts of life at large.

One imagines him moving about gaily and
pleasantly among his friends and fashionable
patients, a privileged guest, carrying his music
with him ; often when he came to prescribe,
remaining to try over some new air, or recit-
some new epigram :

" I to whose trust and care you durst commit
Your pinéd health, when art despaired of it,

.   .   .   .

Should I, for all your ancient love to me,
Endowed with weighty favours, silent be ?
Your merits and my gratitude forbid
That either should in Lethean gulf lie hid ;
But how shall I this work of fame express?
How can I better, after pensiveness,
Than with light strains of Music, made to move
Sweetly with the wide spreading plumes of Love ? "

These lines were addressed to one of his
patients,—" my honourable friend, Sir Thomas
Mounson, Knight and Baronet ; " and the
coupling in them of the arts of medicine and
music is characteristic. Sir Thomas Mounson,
or Monson, had been imprisoned in the Tower
prior to this, in 1615-16, on suspicion of being
concerned in the murder of Sir Thomas Over-
bury. Campion, who had already been of
service in conveying money to him, and was
examined as a friendly witness before his im-
prisonment, was still allowed to visit him in the
Tower, as his medical attendant. The lines

Introduction.

quoted, acclaiming his release, appeared at the opening of the Third Book of Airs, published in 1617 or thereabouts.

This is comparatively far on in his career. The music-book in which he makes what is practically his first appearance as a lyric poet, and in which he had Philip Rosseter as a musical collaborator and editor, appeared about 1601. Campion, then, may be said to emerge with the seventeenth century; and the opening of the seventeenth century comprised some of the goldenest years in all English poetry,—the bridge between Elizabethan and Jacobean times.

In 1601 Spenser had been dead some three years; Sidney some fifteen. Greene, Peele, Marlowe, were gone; Lyly, Lodge, Sir Walter Raleigh, Chapman, Drayton, were alive; and they lead us on to Shakespeare and Ben Jonson. To Ben Jonson, who was at once the last of the Elizabethans and the first of the Jacobeans, succeed the familiar names of the seventeenth century. Campion, like Ben Jonson, though in his different way, is a bridge between the two periods.

This position of his in the chain of English poetry, as one of the few silver links which are purely lyrical, is not of a fanciful importance. He came after the great outburst of Elizabethan energy, and before the classic influence had taught our natural English note too artificial a grace. Nature and art are as happily balanced in Campion as in Herrick; and if he is less impulsive and less inevitable in airy

Introduction.

clearness of lyric style, he has his other qualities, as we may see when he achieves an imaginative flight like,

" When thou must home to shades of underground,
 And there arriv'd, a newe admired guest,
 The beauteous spirits do engirt thee round,
 White Iope, blith Hellen, and the rest,
 To heare the stories of thy finisht love
 From that smoothe toong whose musicke hell can
 move ; "

or a cadence, haunting and mysterious :

" Where are all thy beauties now, all harts enchain-
 ing ?
Whither are thy flatt'rers gone with all their fayning ?
All fled, and thou alone still here remayning ! "

Again, Campion came, as Mr Gosse re-
minded the present editor, before the clearer
waters of English poetry were disturbed by
the masterful irruption of Donne. Donne was
a Welshman on his father's side, and he had
something of the eccentric fire that has so often
made the men of that mixed blood dynamic
and unaccountable, or even lawless, like the
inimitable Jack Mytton in another fashion
altogether.   At any rate, Donne made so
great an effect, that one is almost tempted
to divide the seventeenth century men into
pre-Donne and post-Donne poets. Campion,
fortunately, was a Pre-Donnean ; though what
with his musical sentiment, and his feeling for
a Latin art of verse, he would probably in any
case have held his own, and preserved his
individual note unspoilt.

3 b   xvii

Introduction.

His note has been likened now to Fletcher's, now to Carew's; and he does, for a moment, remind one occasionally of the lyrics of his contemporaries. But rarely though his writing is mannered, his note is as unmistakable as Herrick's own, at its best. Campion's worst, like other poets', we may agree to neglect; it is a very small part of the whole.

No doubt something both of the rarer effect in certain of his poems and of the failure of others, is to be laid to his approaching the art of verse as a musician, rather than as a pure and simple poet.

Take as an instance of a lyric which is exquisitely musical, full of turns which could only have occurred to a musician, full of a lurking melody not likely to have been invented by a mere prosodist, this song of three voices from the Masque given by Lord Knowles to Queen Anne :—

" Night as well as brightest day hath her delight,
  Let us then with mirth and music deck the night.
  Never did glad day such store
    Of joy to night bequeath :
  Her stars then adore,
    Both in Heav'n, and here beneath."

One hears the lute and viol accompaniment plainly in this. The long lines and the short call up to the ear, with charming tunefulness, the effect of certain of his songs as performed delightfully at some of Mr Dolmetsch's concerts of old English music.

Or take the seventeenth song in the third Book of Airs :—

Introduction.

" Shall I come, sweet Love, to thee,
  When the ev'ning beames are set ?
Shall 1 not excluded be ?
  Will you finde no fainéd lett ?
Let me not, for pitty, more,
Tell the long houres at your dore."

The last line, as set to music in the original
gets an added effect by dwelling musically on
the first clause—

" Let me not, for pitty, more,
  Tell the long long houres, tel the long houres, at
    your dore ! "

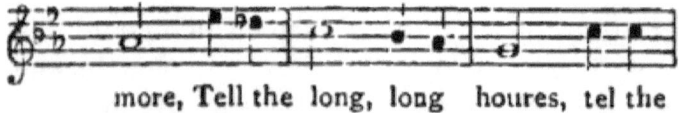

more, Tell the long, long houres, tel the

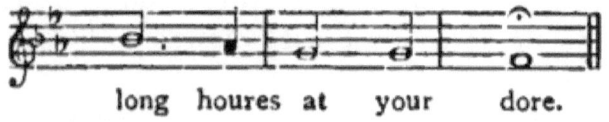

long houres at your dore.

Take another, one of the songs that proved
most effective under Mr Dolmetsch's direction
—the song of Amarillis :—

" I care not for these Ladies,
  That must be woode and praide
Give me kind Amarillis,
The wanton countrey maide.
Nature art disdaineth,
Here beautie is her owne.
  Her when we court and kisse,
  She cries, Forsooth, let go :
  But when we come where comfort is,
  She never will say No."

Introduction.

This is the simple perfection of song-writing. The rhythm, as poetry, is no more charming than the cadence, as music. The words are as lyrical, the movement as impulsive, as anything in Burns or in Shakespeare. It is finely Elizabethan on the face of it, and it is as clearly a song to be sung: a masterpiece-in-little, then, in its own particular kind.

As an instance of what writing for music, without a sufficiently present feeling for poetry, may lead to, take this verse from another song—

" Though far from joy, my sorrows are as far,
   And I both between ;
 Not too low, nor yet too high
 Above my reach would I be seen.
 Happy is he that so is placed,
 Not to be envied nor to be disdained or disgraced."

It is fair to admit that these words were written for Rosseter's setting, not for Campion's own ; and evidently he wrote in this perfunctorily enough.

We turn now for a few moments to glean what we can of Campion's rather paradoxical attitude toward his art of poetry. For it is one of the ironies of literature, that the writer who has written some of the most purely artistic rhymed lyrics in the language,—the most artistic, that is, in the exact sense of lyrical,—should have set out with so striking a manifesto against rhyme. His "Observations in the Art of English Poesie" appeared in 1602, when he had already written some of his loveliest songs.

Introduction.

"I am not ignorant," he says, at the opening
of his second chapter, "that whosoever shall
by way of reprehension examine the imperfec-
tions of Rime, must encounter with many
glorious enemies, and those very expert, and
ready at their weapon, that can if neede be
extempore (as they say) rime a man to death."

Campion the pamphleteer has for enemy
Campion the rhymer; his own songs are the
best reply to his own indictment. Especially
may one quote him against himself, where he
says, and truly :

"The eare is a rationall sence, and a chiefe
judge of proportion, but in our kind of riming
what proportion is there kept where there remaines such a confus'd inequalitie of sillables?"

But the metrical confusion of which he speaks
is as far from the true rhymer as from the
classic poets who never used rhyme. More
finely ordered lyric metres, indeed, we need not
seek than Campion's own. And in spite of
some charming numbers, such as "Rose
Check'd Laura," and his other trochaic lyric,
"Follow, Follow!" in the same lady's honour,
which he produces in this pamphlet to prove
his case; it must be admitted that Campion is
a better poet rhyming, than unrhyming.

However, after allowing for all that is in-
consistent and without argument in his attack,
enough remains to make it a singularly ap-
petising dish in the symposium of the poets in
celebration of their own art. It leaves one as
devoted as ever to "the childish titillation of
riming," as he calls it; especially if read, as it

Introduction.

ought to be, in a sequence with Daniel's admirable reply. Moreover it has many practical points to make as to the technique of verse, which are well worth reading, as springing from so good a verse-writer.

A companion tract in music, though constructive and not destructive in its original scheme, was Campion's "New Way of Making Fowre Parts in Counter-point, by a most familiar and infallible Rule." Mr Bullen did not reprint it in his volume; but it is an interesting production, and, at moments, to others than musicians. One comes on some memorable sentences; as for example, "there is no tune that can have any grace or sweetnesse, unlesse it be bounded within a proper key." This recalls again that feeling for the propriety of word and note, which Campion showed in his practice in both arts.

Some of Campion's prettiest songs are to be found in his masques, which are exquisite in their kind, as full of picturesque effects as of lyrical moments. Indeed, the defect in some of them may have been thought by those who were not musically inclined, that Campion too often interrupted the spectacle in his eagerness to gain yet another lyric opportunity. The first and best of these masques, that performed at the marriage of Lord Hayes (Sir James Hay), we have appended to the present volume. This was certainly much the most lyrical of the four that Campion wrote; he seemed to learn, by his practice in masque-writing, to become less lyrical and to

Introduction.

leave more to the skilled scenic art of his collaborators as he went on. The "Lord Hayes" masque was performed at Whitehall on Twelfth night, 1606-7. We do not come upon another masque of Campion's until six years later, in 1613, when he wrote three. The first was the Lord's Masque, "presented in the Banqueting House on the marriage night of the High and Mighty Count Palatine, and the royally descended the Lady Elizabeth." This, though it was not much praised, by some of its spectators at any rate, is full of taking, and often very splendid, spectacle; which we owe, like the spectacular effect in the best of Ben Jonson's masques, to the genius of Inigo Jones.

Mr Bullen, commenting upon the adverse criticism in one of Chamberlain's letters, which speaks of devices, "long and tedious," "more like a play than a masque," says—

"It is to be noticed that Chamberlain himself was not present; he wrote merely from hear-say. The star dance arranged by Inigo Jones was surely most effective; and the hearers must have been indeed insensate if they were not charmed by the beautiful song, 'Advance your choral motions now.'"

Another of the masques of that year was produced by Lord Knowles (Sir Wm. Knollys), at Cawsam (Caversham) House, Reading, in honour of "our most gracious Queene, Queene Anne, in her Progresse toward the Bathe," on the 27th and 28th April 1613. The third was that produced for the marriage of the Earl of

Introduction.

Somerset and "the infamous Lady Frances
Howard, the divorced Countess of Essex," on
the 26th December 1613.

In the same year Campion again showed
his close connection with the Court by the
little volume, "Songs of Mourning," in memory
of the untimely death of Prince Henry, in
November 1612. The songs, in which Campion
was not altogether inspired, were set to music
by Coprario (*alias* John Cooper). But else-
where, in his "Divine and Moral Songs,"
Campion showed how well he could turn his
lyric note to a grave measure. Indeed, he
passed with ease and grace from such impulsive ditties as Amarillis to such solemn
songs as "Lift up to Heav'n, sad wretch,
thy Heavy spright!" or those two touching
stanzas, beginning :

"Never weather beaten Saile more willing bent to
    shore,
 Never tyred Pilgrim's limbs affected slumber
    more."

One finds, after reading Campion with anything like sympathy, that he leaves the memory
wonderfully replenished with such things,—
things far too tender, witty, or true ; too rare,
rich, and fine, to be ever forgotten. In purely
lyric poetry, he is, perhaps, the most remark-
able discovery of our time amid the dust of
old libraries, tireless as our zeal of research
has been. He is, in brief, a master in his
own field ; and that field as widely, or as

Introduction.

narrowly, determined in its lyric bounds as you care to make it.

The present edition of Campion,—the first in which he has made full public entrance before the wider audience,—owes, let me add, the fullest acknowledgment to the previous labours of Mr A. H. Bullen; to whose courtesy in waiving his claim upon a poet that he had almost made his own, the reader, as well as the editor, of the volume, must remain thrice indebted. For the most part Campion's original text is, however, here made use of; in the contrary case, as in the Masque at the end, Mr Bullen's initials will be found attached.

E. R.

November, 1895.

To the Reader.

Campion's Preface to Rosseter's "Book of Ayres" (1601).

WHAT Epigrams are in Poetrie, the same are Ayres in musicke: then in their chiefe perfection when they are short and well seasoned. But to clogg a light song with a long Præludium, is to corrupt the nature of it. Manie rests in Musicke were invented, either for necessitie of the fuge, or granted as a harmonicall licence in songs of many parts: but in Ayres I find no use they have, unlesse it be to make a vulgar and triviall modulation seeme to the ignorant, strange; and to the judiciall, tedious. A naked Ayre without guide, or prop, or colour but his owne, is easily censured of everie ear; and requires so much the more invention to make it please. And as Martiall speakes in defence of his short Epigrams; so may I say in th' apologie of Ayres: that where there is a full volume, there can be no imputation of shortnes. The Lyricke Poets among the Greekes and Latines were first inventers of Ayres, tying themselves strictly to the number and value of their sillables: of which sort, you shall find here onely one song in Saphicke verse; the rest are after the fascion of the time, eare-pleasing rimes without Arte. The subject of them is, for

the most part amorous; and why not amorous songs, as well as amorous attires? Or
why not new airs, as well as new fascions?
For the Note and Tableture, if they satisfie
the most, we have our desire; let expert
masters please themselves with better. And
if anie light error hath escaped us, the skilfull may easily correct it, the unskilfull will
hardly perceive it. But there are some who,
to appeare the more deepe and singular in
their judgement, will admit no Musicke but
that which is long, intricate, bated with fuge,
chaind with sincopation, and where the nature
of everie word is precisely exprest in the Note:
like the old exploided action in Comedies, when
if they did pronounce Memeni, they would
point to the hinder part of their heads; if
Video, put their finger in their eye. But such
childish observing of words is altogether ridicu-
lous; and we ought to maintaine, as well in
notes as in action, a manly cariage; gracing
no word, but that which is eminent and
emphaticall. Nevertheles, as in Poesie we
give the preheminence to the Heroicall Poem;
so in musicke, we yield the chiefe place to
the grave and well invented Motet: but not
to every harsh and dull confused Fantasie,
where, in multitude of points, the Harmonie
is quite drowned. Ayres have both their Art
and pleasure: and I will conclude of them,
as the poet did in his censure of Catullus the
Lyricke, and Vergil the Heroicke writer:

Tantum magna suo debet Verona Catullo,
Quantum parva suo Mantua Vergilio.

Campion.

To the Reader.

Preface to the "Two Bookes of Ayres" (1613?).

Out of many Songs which, partly at the equest of friends, partly for my owne recreation, were by mee long since composed, I have now enfranchised a few; sending them forth divided, according to the different subject into severall Bookes. The first are grave and pious; the second, amorous and light. For hee that in publishing any worke hath a desire to content all palates, must cater for them accordingly.

Non omnibus unum est
Quod placet, hic Spinas colligit, ille Rosas.

These Ayres were for the most part framed at first for one voyce with the Lute or Violl: but upon occasion they have since beene filled with more parts, which whoso please may use, who like not may leave. Yet doe wee daily observe that when any shall sing a Treble to an instrument, the standers by will be offring at an inward part out of their owne nature; and, true or false, out it must, though to the perverting of the whole harmonie. Also, if wee consider well, the Treble tunes (which are with us, commonly called Ayres) are but Tenors mounted eight Notes higher; and therefore an inward part must needes well become them, such as may take up the whole distance of the

Diapason, and fill up the gaping betweene the two extreeme parts; whereby though they are not three parts in perfection, yet they yeeld a sweetnesse and content both to the eare and minde; which is the ayme and perfection of Musicke. Short Ayres, if they be skilfully framed, and naturally exprest are like quicke and good Epigrames in Poesie; many of them shewing as much artifice, and breeding as great difficultie as a larger Poeme. *Non omnia possumus omnes*, said the Romane Epicke Poet. But some there are who admit onely French or Italian Ayres; as if every Country had not his proper Ayre, which the people thereof naturally usurpe in their Musicke. Others taste nothing that comes forth in print; as if Catullus or Martial's Epigrammes were the worse for being published.

In these English Ayres, I have chiefely aymed to couple my Words and Notes lovingly together; which will be much for him to doe that hath not power over both. The light of this, will best appeare to him who hath pays'd our Monasyllables and Syllables combined: both which are so loaded with Consonants as that they will hardly keepe company with swift Notes, or give the Vowell convenient liberty.

To conclude; mine own opinion of these Songs I deliver thus:

Omnia nec nostris bona sunt, sed nec mala libris;
    Si placet hac cantes, hac quoq'. lege legas.
                                    Farewell.

Dedication of "Light Conceits of Lovers" (1613?).

"To the Right Noble and Vertuous Henry, Lord Clifford, sonne and heyre to the Right Honourable Francis, Earle of Cumberland."

SUCH dayes as wear the badge of holy red
   Are for devotion markt and sage delight;
The vulgar Low-dayes, undistinguished,
   Are left for labour, games, and sportfull
     sights.

This sev'rall and so differing use of Time,
   Within th' enclosure of one weeke wee finde;
Which I resemble in my Notes and Rhyme,
   Expressing both in their peculiar kinde.

Pure Hymnes, such as the seaventh day loves,
     doe leade;
   Grave age did justly chalenge those of
     mee:
These weekeday workes, in order that suc-
     ceede,
Your youth best fits; and yours, yong Lord,
     they be,
As hee is, who to them their beeing gave:
If th' one, the other you of force must have.

—ᶺᴧᴧᴧ—

" THE Apothecaries have Bookes of Gold, whose leaves, being opened, are so light as that they are subject to be shaken with the least breath ; yet rightly handled, they serve both for ornament and use : such are light Ayres."   CAMPION.

Now Winter Nights Enlarge.

Third Booke of Ayres.
(1617?). "Hunny" (l.
10), honey.

Now winter nights enlarge
The number of their houres ;
And clouds their stormes discharge
Upon the ayrie towres
Let now the chimneys blaze
And cups o'erflow with wine,
Let well-tun'd words amaze
With harmonie divine !
Now yellow waxen lights
Shall waite on hunny love
While youthfull Revels, Masks, and Courtly
      sights,
Sleepe's leaden spels remove.

  This time doth well dispence
  With lovers' long discourse ;
Much speech hath some defence,
  Though beauty no remorse.
All doe not all things well ;
  Some measures comely tread,
Some knotted Ridles tell,
  Some Poems smoothly read.
The Summer hath his joyes,
  And Winter his delights ;
Though Love and all his pleasures are but
      toyes,
  They shorten tedious nights,

Cherry Ripe.

Fourth Booke of Ayres (1617 ?).

THERE is a Garden in her face,
Where Roses and white Lillies grow ;
A heav'nly paradice is that place,
Wherein all pleasant fruits doe flow.
There Cherries grow, which none may buy
Till Cherry ripe themselves do cry.

Those Cherries fayrely doe enclose
Of Orient Pearle a double row ;
Which when her lovely laughter showes,
They look like Rose-buds fill'd with snow.
Yet them nor Peere nor Prince can buy
Till Cherry ripe themselves doe cry.

Her Eyes like Angels watch them still ;
Her Browes like bended bowes doe stand,
Threatning with piercing frownes to kill
All that attempt, with eye or hand,
Those sacred Cherries to come nigh,
Till Cherry ripe themselves do cry.

—ᴧᴧᴧ—

When to her Lute.

Rosseter's Ayres. Part I. (1601).

WHEN to her lute Corinna sings,
Her voice revives the leaden stringes,
And doth in highest noates appeare,
As any challeng'd eccho cleere ;

2

But when she doth of mourning speake,
Ev'n with her sighes the strings do breake.

And as her lute doth live or die,
Led by her passion, so must I ;
For when of pleasure, she doth sing,
My thoughts enjoy a sodaine spring ;
But if she doth of sorrow speake,
Ev'n from my heart the strings do breake.

—/\/\/\—

Sleepe, Angry Beauty.

Third Book of Ayres (1617?).

SLEEPE, angry beauty, sleepe, and feare not
  me.
  For who a sleeping Lyon dares provoke ?
It shall suffice me here to sit and see
  Those lips shut up, that never kindely spoke.
What sight can more content a lover's minde
Then beauty seeming harmlesse, if not kinde ?

My words have charm'd her, for secure shee
    sleepes ;
  Though guilty much of wrong done to my
    love ;
And in her slumber, see, shee, close-ey'd, weepes !
  Dreames often more than waking passions
    move.
Pleade, Sleepe, my cause, and make her soft
    like thee,
That shee in peace may wake and pitty mee.

3

Never Love Unless You Can.

Third Booke of Ayres (1617?).

Never love unlesse you can
Beare with all the faults of man :
Men sometimes will jealous bee,
Though but little cause they see ;
And hang the head, as discontent,
And speake what straight they will
    repent.

Men that but one saint adore,
Make a show of love to more :
Beauty must be scorn'd in none,
Though but truly serv'd in one :
For what is courtship, but disguise?
True hearts may have dissembling eyes.

Men when their affaires require,
Must a while themselves retire :
Sometimes hunt, and sometimes hawke,
And not ever sit and talke.
If these, and such like you can beare,
Then like, and love, and never feare !

—vvv—

So Quicke, so Hot.

Third Booke of Ayres (1617?).

So quicke, so hot, so mad is thy fond suit,
  So rude, so tedious growne, in urging mee,
That fain I would, with losse, make thy tongue
      mute,
    And yeeld some little grace to quiet thee :
An houre with thee I care not to converse,
For I would not be counted too perverse.

But roofes too hot would prove for men all fire ;
  And hills too high for my unused pace ;
The grove is charg'd with thornes and the bold
      bryar ;
    Grey snakes the meadowes shroude in every
      place :
A yellow frog, alas, will fright me so,
As I should start and tremble as I goe.

Since then I can on earth no fit roome finde,
  In heaven I am resolv'd with you to meete :
Till then, for Hope's sweet sake, rest your tir'd
      minde
    And not so much as see mee in the streete :
A heavenly meeting one day wee shall have,
But never, as you dreame, in bed, or grave.

—∿∿∿—

Though you are Yoong.

Rosseter's Booke of Ayres. Part I. (1601).

THOUGH you are yoong, and I am olde,
Though your vaines hot, and my bloud colde,
Though youth is moist, and age is drie;
Yet embers live, when flames doe die.

The tender graft is easely broke,
But who shall shake the sturdie Oke?
You are more fresh and fair then I;
Yet stubs doe live, when flowers doe die.

Thou, that thy youth doest vainely boast,
Know buds are soonest nipt with frost:
Thinke that thy fortune still doth crie,
Thou foole, to-morrow thou must die!

Thou art not Faire.

Rosseter's Booke o, Ayres. Part I. (1601).

Thou art not faire, for all thy red and white,
For all those rosie ornaments in thee ;
Thou art not sweet, though made of nicer
  delight,
Nor faire nor sweet, unless thou pitie me.
I will not sooth thy fancies : thou shalt prove
That beauty is no beautie without love.

Yet love not me, nor seeke thou to allure
My thoughts with beautie, were it more devine :
Thy smiles and kisses I cannot endure,
I'le not be wrapt up in those armes of thine :
Now show it, if thou be a woman right,—
Embrace, and kisse, and love me, in despight !

—◠◠◠—

When thou must Home.

Rosseter's Booke of Ayres. Part I. (1601).

When thou must home to shades of under-
  ground,
And there arriv'd, a newe admired guest,
The beauteous spirits do ingirt thee round,
White Iope, blith Hellen, and the rest,
To heare the stories of thy finisht love,
From that smoothe toong whose musicke hell
  can move ;

Then wilt thou speake of banqueting delights,
Of masks and revels which sweete youth did
    make,
Of Turnies and great challenges of knights,
And all these triumphes for thy beauties sake :
When thou hast told these honours done to
    thee,
Then tell, O tell, how thou didst murther me.

—∿∿∿—

Shall I Come, Sweet Love.

Third Booke of Ayres (1617 ?).

SHALL I come, sweet love, to thee,
    When the evening beames are set ?
Shall I not excluded be ?
    Will you finde no fained lett ?
Let me not, for pitty, more,
Tell the long houres at your dore !

Who can tell what theefe or foe,
    In the covert of the night,
For his prey will worke my woe,
    Or through wicked foul despite ?
So may I dye unredrest,
Ere my long love be possest.

But to let such dangers passe,
    Which a lover's thoughts disdaine,
'Tis enough in such a place
    To attend love's joyes in vaine.
Doe not mocke me in thy bed,
While these cold nights freeze me dead.

Awake, thou Spring.

Third Booke of Ayres (1617 ?).

AWAKE, thou spring of speaking grace,
    mute rest becomes not thee !
The fayrest women, while they sleepe, and
    pictures, equall bee.
  O come and dwell in love's discourses,
    Old renuing, new creating.
  The words which thy rich tongue discourses,
    Are not of the common rating !

Thy voyce is as an Eccho cleare, which Musicke
    doth beget,
Thy speech is as an Oracle, which none can
    counterfeit :
  For thou alone, without offending,
    Hast obtained power of enchanting ;
  And I could heare thee without ending,
    Other comfort never wanting.

Some little reason brutish lives with humane
    glory share ;
But language is our proper grace, from which
    they sever'd are.
  As brutes in reason man surpasses,
    Men in speech excell each other :
  If speech be then the best of graces,
    Doe it not in slumber smother !

Amarillis.

Rosseter. Part I.
(1601).

I CARE not for these Ladies,
That must be wooed and praide :
Give me kind Amarillis,
The wanton countrey maide.
Nature art disdaineth,
Her beautie is her owne.
    Her when we court and kisse,
    She cries, Forsooth, let go :
    But when we come where comfort is,
    She never will say No.

If I love Amarillis,
She gives me fruit and flowers : ·
But if we love these Ladies,
We must give golden showers.
Give them gold that sell love,
Give me the Nut-browne lasse,
    Who, when we court and kisse,
    She cries, Forsooth, let go :
    But when we come where comfort is,
    She never will say No.

These Ladies must have pillowes,
And beds by strangers wrought ;
Give me a Bower of willows,
Of mosse and leaves unbought,
And fresh Amarillis,
With milk and honie fed ;
    Who, when we court and kisse,
    She cries Forsooth, let go :
    But when we come where comfort is,
    She never will say No !

Mistris, since you so much Desire.

Rosseter. Part I.
(1601).

Mistris, since you so much desire
To know the place of Cupid's fire,
In your faire shrine that flame doth rest,
Yet never harbourd in your brest.
It bides not in your lips so sweete,
Nor where the rose and lillies meete;
But a little higher, but a little higher
There, there, O there lies Cupid's fire.

Even in those starrie pearcing eyes,
There Cupid's sacred fire lyes.
Those eyes I strive not to enjoy,
For they have power to destroy;
Nor woe I for a smile or kisse,
So meanely triumphs not my blisse;
But a little higher, but a little higher,
I climbe to crowne my chaste desire.

—⁓⋀⋀⋁⋁⋯—

Turne backe you Wanton Flier.

Rosseter. Part I.
(1601).

Turne backe, you wanton flier
And answere my desire,
With mutuall greeting:
Yet bende a little neerer,

True beauty still shines cleerer,
In closer meeting.
Harts with harts delighted,
Should strive to be united ;
Either other's armes with armes enchayning :
Harts with a thought,
Rosie lips with a kisse still entertaining.
What harvest halfe so sweete is
As still to reape the kisses
Growne ripe in sowing?
And straight to be receiver
Of that which thou art giver,
Rich in bestowing?
There's no strickt observing
Of times, or seasons changing ;
There is ever one fresh spring abiding.
Then what we sow with our lips,
Let us reape, love's gaines deviding !

—∿∿∿—

So Sweet is thy Discourse.

Fourth Booke of Ayres (1617 ?).

So sweet is thy discourse to me,
And so delightfull is thy sight,
As I taste nothing right but thee.
O why invented Nature light?
Was it alone for beauties sake,
That her grac't words might better take?

Campion.

No more can I old joyes recall :
They now to me become unknowne,
Not seeming to have beene at all.
Alas ! how soone is this love growne
To such a spreading height in me
As with it all must shadowed be !

—⁓W⁓—

To his Sweet Lute Apollo sung.

Fourth Booke of Ayres (1617 ?).

To his sweet lute Apollo sung the motions of
    the Spheares ;
The wondrous order of the Stars, whose course
    divides the yeares ;
      And all the Mysteries above :
      But none of this could Midas move,
    Which purchast him his Asses eares.

Then Pan with his rude pipe began the Coun-
    try-wealth t'advance,
To boast of Cattle, flocks of Sheepe, and Goates
    on hils that dance ;
      With much more of this churlish kinde,
      That quite transported Midas mind,
    And held him rapt as in a trance.

This wrong the God of Musicke scorn'd from
    such a sottish Judge,
And bent his angry brow at Pan, which made
    the Piper trudge :

Then Midas' head he so did trim,
That ev'ry age yet talkes of him,
And Phœbus right revenged grudge.

—ᴡᴧᴧᴧ—

To Musicke Bent. Divine and Morall Songs (1613 ?).

To Musicke bent, is my retyred minde,
   And faine would I some song of pleasure sing ;
But in vaine joyes no comfort now I finde,
   From heav'nly thoughts all true delight doth
      spring :
Thy power, O God, thy mercies to record,
Will sweeten ev'ry note and ev'ry word.

All earthly pompe or beauty to expresse,
   Is but to carve in snow, on waves to write ;
Celestiall things, though men conceive them
      lesse,
   Yet fullest are they in themselves of light :
Such beames they yeeld as know no meanes to
      dye,
Such heate they cast as lifts the Spirit high.

Campion.

The Man of Life Upright.

Divine and Morall Songs (1613?).

THE man of life upright,
Whose guiltlesse hart is free
From all dishonest deedes,
Or thought of vanitie ;

The man whose silent dayes,
In harmles joys are spent,
Whome hopes cannot delude
Nor sorrow discontent ;

That man needes neyther towres
Nor armour for defence,
Nor secret vautes to flie
From thunder's violence ;

Hee onely can behold
With unafrighted eyes
The horrours of the deepe
And terrours of the Skies.

Thus, scorning all the cares
That fate or fortune brings,
He makes the heav'n his booke,
His wisedome heav'nly things ;

Good thoughts his onely friendes,
His wealth a well-spent age,
The earth his sober Inne
And quiet Pilgrimage.

Where are all thy Beauties now, all Harts enchaining?

Divine and Morall Songs (1613 ?).

WHERE are all thy beauties now, all harts
    enchaining?
Whither are thy flatt'rers gone with all their
    fayning?
All fled, and thou alone still here remayning!

Thy rich state of twisted gold to Bayes is
    turned!
Cold as thou art, are thy loves that so much
    burned!
Who dye in flatt'rers' armes are seldome
    mourned.

Yet in spite of envie, this be still proclaymed,
That none worthyer then thyselfe thy worth
    hath blamed;
When their poore names are lost, thou shalt
    live famed.

When thy story long time hence shall be per-
    used,
Let the blemish of thy rule be thus excused,—
None ever liv'd more just, none more abused.

Come, chearfull Day.

COME, chearfull day, part of my life, to mee :
  For while thou view'st me with thy fading light,
Part of my life doth still depart with thee,
  And I still onward haste to my last night.
Time's fatall wings doe ever forward flye :
So ev'ry day we live, a day wee dye.

But, O yee nights, ordained for barren rest,
  How are my dayes depriv'd of life in you,
When heavy sleepe my soul hath dispossest,
  By fayned death life sweetly to renew !
Part of my life in that you life denye :
So ev'ry day we live a day wee dye.

—\/\/\/\—

Awake, Awake.

AWAKE, awake, thou heavy spright,
  That sleep'st the deadly sleepe of sinne !
Rise now and walke the wayes of light !
  'Tis not too late yet to begin.
Seeke heav'n earely, secke it late :
True Faith still findes an open gate.

Get up, get up, thou leaden man !
   Thy tracks to endlesse joy, or paine
Yeeld but the modell of a span ;
   Yet burnes out thy life's lampe in vaine !
One minute bounds thy bane, or blisse :
Then watch, and labour while time is !

—wWw—

Followe thy faire Sunne.

Rosseter.   Part I.
(1601).

FOLLOWE thy faire sunne, unhappy shaddowe,
Though thou be blacke as night,
And she made all of light,
Yet follow thy faire sunne, unhappie shaddowe !

Follow her whose light thy light depriveth ;
Though here thou liv'st disgrae't,
And she in heaven is plac't,
Yet follow her whose light the world reviveth.

Follow those pure beames whose beautie
    burneth,
That so have scorched thee,
As thou still blacke must bee,
Til her kind beames thy black to brightnes
    turneth.

Follow her while yet her glorie shineth :
There comes a luckles night,
That will dim all her light ;
And this the black unhappie shade devineth.

Follow still since so thy fates ordained ;
The Sunne must have his shade,
Till both at once doe fade ;
The sun still prov'd, the shadow still disdained.

—∿∿∿—

And would you see my Mistris' Face ?

Rosseter's Booke of Ayres. Part II. (1601)

AND would you see my Mistris' face?
It is a flowrie garden place,
Where knots of beauties have such grace,
That all is worke and nowhere space.

It is a sweete delicious morne,
Where day is breeding, never borne ;
It is a Meadow yet unshorne,
Whom thousand flowers do adorne.

It is the heaven's bright reflexe,
Weake eies to dazle and to vexe :
It is th' Idæa of her sexe,
Envie of whome doth worlds perplexe.

It is a face of death that smiles,
Pleasing, though it killes the whiles :
Where death and love in pretie wiles
Each other mutuallie beguiles.

It is faire beautie's freshest youth,
It is the fained Elizium's truth :
The spring, that winter'd harts renu'th ;
And this is that my soule pursu'th.

—\/\/\/\—

Vaine Men, whose Follies.

Light   Conceits   of
Lovers (1613?).

Vaine men, whose follies make a God of
    Love,
Whose blindnesse beauty doth immortall deeme;
Prayse not what you desire, but what you
    prove,
Count those things good that are, not those
    that seeme :
I cannot call her true that's false to me,
Nor make of women more than women be.

How fair an entrance breakes the way to love !
How rich of golden hope, and gay delight !
What hart cannot a modest beauty move ?
Who, seeing cleare day once, will dreame of
    night ?
She seem'd a Saint, that brake her faith with
    mee,
But prov'd a woman as all other be.

So bitter is their sweet, that true content
Unhappy men in them may never finde :
Ah, but without them none.   Both must con-
    sent,
Else uncouth are the joyes of eyther kinde.
Let us then prayse their good, forget their ill !
Men must be men, and women women still.

—vvv—

How eas'ly wert thou Chained.

Light   Conceits   of
Lovers (1613?).

How eas'ly wert thou chained,
Fond hart, by favours fained !
Why liv'd thy hopes in grace,
Straight to die disdained ?
But since th' art now beguiled
By Love that falsely smiled,
In some lesse happy place
Mourne alone exiled !
My love still here increaseth,
And with my love my griefe,
While her sweet bounty ceaseth,
That gave my woes reliefe.
Yet 'tis no woman leaves me,
For such may prove unjust ;
A Goddesse thus deceives me
Whose faith who could mistrust ?
A Goddesse so much graced,
That Paradice is placed

In her most heav'nly brest,
Once by love embraced :
But love, that so kind proved,
Is now from her removed,
Nor will he longer rest
Where no faith is loved.
If Powres Celestiall wound us
And will not yeeld reliefe,
Woe then must needs confound us,
For none can cure our grief.
No wonder if I languish
Through burden of my smart,
It is no common anguish
From Paradice to part.

—∧∧∨∨∧—

Harden now thy tyred Hart.

Light Conceits of Lovers (1613?).

HARDEN now thy tyred hart with more then
flinty rage !
Ne'er let her false teares henceforth thy constant griefe asswage !
Once true happy dayes thou saw'st when shee
stood firme and kinde,
Both as one then liv'd and held one eare, one
tongue, one minde :
But now those bright houres be fled, and never
may returne ;
What then remaines but her untruths to
mourne ?

Campion.

Silly Trayt'resse, who shall now thy carelesse
   tresses place?
Who thy pretty talke supply? whose eare thy
   musicke grace?
Who shall thy bright eyes admire? what lips
   triumph with thine?
Day by day who'll visit thee, and say: Th'art
   onely mine?
Such a time there was, God wot, but such
   shall never be:
Too oft, I feare, thou wilt remember me.

—◇◇◇—

O what Unhop't for Sweet Supply.

Light Conceits of Lovers (1613?).

O WHAT unhop't for sweet supply!
   O what joyes exceeding!
What an affecting charme feele I,
   From delight proceeding!
That which I long despair'd to be,
To her I am, and shee to mee.

Shee that alone in cloudy griefe
   Long to mee appeared:
Shee now alone with bright reliefe
   All those clouds hath cleared.
Both are immortall and divine,
Since I am hers, and she is mine.

23

Where Shee her Sacred Bowre Adornes.

Light   Conceits   of
Lovers (1613?).

WHERE shee her sacred bowre adornes,
  The Rivers clearely flow ;
The groves and medowes swell with flowres
  The windes all gently blow.
Her Sunne-like beauty shines so fayre,
  Her Spring can never fade :
Who then can blame the life that strives
  To harbour in her shade ?

Her grace I sought, her love I wooed,
  Her love though I obtaine ;
No time, no toyle, no vow, no faith,
  Her wished grace can gaine.
Yet truth can tell my heart is hers,
  And her will I adore ;
And from that love when I depart,
  Let heav'n view me no more !

Her roses with my prayes shall spring ;
  And when her trees I praise,
Their boughs shall blossome, mellow fruit
  Shall straw her pleasant wayes.
The words of harty zeale have powre
  High wonders to effect ;
O why should then her princely eare
  My words, or zeale, neglect ?

Campion.

If shee my faith misdeemes, or worth,
  Woe worth my haplesse fate !
For though time can my truth reveale,
  That time will come too late.
And who can glory in the worth,
  That cannot yeeld him grace ?
Content, in ev'rything is not,
  Nor joy in ev'ry place.

But from her bowre of Joy since I
  Must now excluded be,
And shee will not relieve my cares,
  Which none can helpe but shee ;
My comfort in her love shall dwell,
  Her love lodge in my brest,
And though not in her bowre, yet I
  Shall in her temple rest.

—✲✲✲—

Faine would I My Love Disclose.

Light   Conceits   of
Lovers (1613 ?).

Faine would I my love disclose,
Aske what honour might denye ;
But both love and her I lose,
From my motion if shee flye.
Worse then paine is feare to mee :
Then hold in fancy though it burne ;
If not happy, safe I'le be,
And to my clostred cares returne.

25

Lyric Poems.

Yet, O yet, in vaine I strive
To represse my school'd desire ;
More and more the flames revive,
I consume in mine owne fire.
She would pitty, might shee know
The harmes that I for her endure :
Speake then, and get comfort so ;
A wound long hid growes past recure.

Wise shee is, and needs must know
All th' attempts that beauty moves ;
Fayre she is, and honour'd so
That she, sure, hath tryed some loves.
If with love I tempt her then,
'Tis but her due to be desir'd :
What would women thinke of men,
If their deserts were not admir'd ?

Women courted have the hand
To discard what they distaste :
But those Dames whom none demand
Want oft what their wils imbrac't.
Could their firmnesse iron excell,
As they are faire, they should be sought :
When true theeves use falsehood well,
As they are wise, they will be caught.

—◦◦◦—

Give Beauty All Her Right.

Light Conceits of Lovers (1613?).

Gɪᴠᴇ beauty all her right,
She's not to one forme tyed ;
Each shape yeelds faire delight,
Where her perfections bide.
Hellen, I grant, might pleasing be ;
And Ros'mond was as sweet as shee.

Some, the quicke eye commends ;
Some, swelling lips and red ;
Pale lookes have many friends,
Through sacred sweetnesse bred.
Medowes have flowres that pleasure move,
Though Roses are the flowres of love.

Free beauty is not bound
To one unmoved clime :
She visits ev'ry ground,
And favours ev'ry time.
Let the old loves with mine compare,
My Sov'raigne is as sweet and fair.

—ᴡᴡ—

O Deare! that I with Thee might Live.

Light Conceits of
Lovers (1612 ?).

O DEARE, that I with thee might live,
    From humane trace removed !
Where jealous care might neither grieve,
    Yet each dote on their loved.
While fond feare may colour finde, Love's
    seldome pleased ;
But much like a sicke man's rest, it's soone
    diseased.

Why should our mindes not mingle so,
    When love and faith is plighted,
That eyther might the other's know,
    Alike in all delighted ?
Why should frailtie breed suspect, when hearts
    are fixed ?
Must all humane joys of force with griefe be
    mixed ?

How oft have wee ev'n smilde in teares,
    Our fond mistrust repenting ?
As snow when heav'nly fire appeares,
    So melts love's hate relenting.
Vexed kindnesse soone fals off, and soone
    returneth :
Such a flame the more you quench the more it
    burneth.

Campion.

Good Men shew, if You can Tell.
Light Conceits of Lovers (1613?).

Good men shew, if you can tell,
Where doth humane pittie dwell?
Farre and neere her would I seeke
So vext with sorrow is my brest:
She, (they say) to all, is meeke;
And onely makes th' unhappie blest.

Oh! if such a Saint there be,
Some hope yet remaines for me:
Prayer or sacrifice may gaine
From her implored grace reliefe;
To release mee of my paine,
Or at the least to ease my griefe.

Young am I, and farre from guile,
The more is my woe the while:
Falshood with a smooth disguise
My simple meaning hath abus'd:
Casting mists before thine eyes,
By which my senses are confus'd.

Faire he is, who vow'd to me
That he onely mine would be;
But, alas, his minde is caught
With ev'ry gaudie bait he sees:
And too late my flame is taught
That too much kindnesse makes men freese.

29

From me all my friends are gone
While I pine for him alone;
And not one will rue my case,
But rather my distresse deride:
That I thinke there is no place
Where pittie ever yet did bide.

—∿∿∿—

Whether Men doe Laugh or Weepe.

A Booke of Ayres.
Part II. (1601).

WHETHER men doe laugh or weepe,
Whether they doe wake or sleepe,
Whether they die yoong or olde,
Whether they feele heate or colde;
There is, underneath the sunne,
Nothing in true earnest done.

All our pride is but a jest,
None are worst, and none are best,
Griefe, and joy, and hope, and feare,
Play their Pageants everywhere:
Vaine opinion all doth sway,
And the world is but a play.

Powers above in cloudes do sit,
Mocking our poore apish wit;
That so lamely, with such state,
Their high glorie imitate:
No ill can be felt but paine,
And that happie men disdaine

What then is Love but Mourning?

A Booke of Ayres.
Part II. (1601).

WHAT then is love but mourning?
What desire, but a selfe-burning?
Till shee, that hates, doth love returne,
Thus will I mourne, thus will I sing,
    Come away! come away, my darling!

Beautie is but a blooming,
    Youth in his glorie entombing;
Time hath a while which none can stay:
Then come away, while thus I sing,
    Come away! come away, my darling!

Sommer in winter fadeth;
    Gloomie night heav'nly light shadeth:
Like to the morne, are Venus' flowers;
Such are her howers: then will I sing,
    Come away! come away, my darling!

—◇◇◇—

Lyric Poems.

Kinde in Un-kindnesse, when will You relent.

A Booke of Ayres.
Part II. (1601).

KINDE in unkindnesse, when will you relent
And cease with faint love true love to torment ?
Still entertained, excluded still I stand ;
Her glove still holde, but cannot touch the
    hand.

In her faire hand my hopes and comforts rest :
O might my fortunes with that hand be blest !
No envious breaths then my deserts could
    shake,
For they are good whom such true love doth
    make.

O let not beautie so forget her birth,
That it should fruitles home returne to earth !
Love is the fruite of beautie, then love one !
Not your sweete selfe, for such selfe-love is
    none.

Love one that onely lives in loving you ;
Whose wrong'd deserts would you with pity
    view,
This strange distast which your affections
    swaies
Would relish love, and you find better daies.

32

Campion.

Thus till my happie sight your beautie viewes,
Whose sweet remembrance stil my hope
    renewes,
Let these poore lines sollicite love for mee,
And place my joyes where my desires would
    bee.

—◁◁◁◁—

When Laura Smiles.

Rosseter.   Part II.
(1601).—A. H. B.

WHEN Laura smiles her sight revives both
    night and day ;
The earth and heaven views with delight her
    wanton play :
And her speech with ever-flowing music doth
    repair
The cruel wounds of sorrow and untamed
    despair.

The sprites that remain in fleeting air
Affect for pastime to untwine her tressed hair :
And the birds think sweet Aurora, Morning's
    Queen, doth shine
From her bright sphere, when Laura shows
    her looks divine.

Diana's eyes are not adorned with greater
    power
Than Laura's, when she lists awhile for sport
    to lower :

But when she her eyes encloseth, blindness
    doth appear
The chiefest grace of beauty, sweetly seated
    there.

Love hath no power but what he steals from
    her bright eyes ;
Time hath no power but that which in her
    pleasure lies :
For she with her divine beauties all the world
    subdues,
And fills with heavenly spirits my humble
    Muse.

—ᴧᴧᴧᴧ—

Rose-cheeked Laura.

Unrhymed song from "Observations in the Art of English Poesie," 1602. "The number," says Campion, "is voluble, and fit to express any amorous conceit."— A. H. B.

Rose-cheeked Laura, come ;
Sing thou smoothly with thy beauty's
Silent music, either other
    Sweetly gracing.
Lovely forms do flow
From concent divinely framed ;
Heav'n is music, and thy beauty's
    Birth is heavenly.
These dull notes we sing
Discords need for helps to grace them,

Campion.

Only beauty purely loving
        Knows no discord,
But still moves delight,
Like clear springs renewed by flowing,
Ever perfect, ever in them-
        Selves eternal.

— ᜒᜒᜒ —

Scornfull Laura.

Anacreontic from " Ob-
servations in the Art of
English Poesie " (1602).—
A. H. B.

FOLLOW, follow,
Though with mischief
Armed, like whirlwind
Now she flies thee ;
Time can conquer
Love's unkindness ;
Love can alter
Time's disgraces :
Till death faint not
Then, but follow.
Could I catch that
Nimble traitor
Scornful Laura,
Swift-foot Laura,
Soon then would I
Seek avengement.
What's th' avengement ?
Ev'n submissly
Prostrate then to
Beg for mercy.

35

See where She flies enrag'd from Me!

Rosseter.   Part I.
(1601).

See where she flies enrag'd from me !
View her when she intends despite,
The winde is not more swift than shee.
Her furie mov'd such terror makes,
As to a fearfull guiltie sprite,
The voice of heav'ns huge thundercracks :
But when her appeased minde yeelds to delight,
All her thoughts are made of joies,
Millions of delights inventing ;
Other pleasures are but toies
To her beautie's sweet contenting.

My fortune hangs upon her brow ;
For as she smiles, or frownes on mee,
So must my blowne affections bow ;
And her proude thoughts too well do find
With what unequall tyrannie
Her beauties doe command my mind.
Though when her sad planet raignes,
Froward she bee,
She alone can pleasure move,
And displeasing sorrow banish.
May I but still hold her love,
Let all other comforts vanish.

Campion.

Your faire Lookes enflame my Desire.

Rosseter. Part 1.
(1601).

Your faire lookes enflame my desire :
      Quench it againe with love !
Stay, O strive not still to retire :
      Doe not inhumane prove !
If love may perswade,
      Love's pleasures, deare, denie not.
Here is a silent grovie shade ;
      O tarry then, and fly not !

Have I seaz'd my heavenly delight
      In this unhaunted grove ?
Time shall now her furie requite
      With the revenge of love.
Then come, sweetest, come,
      My lips with kisses gracing !
Here let us harbour all alone,
      Die, die in sweete embracing !

Will you now so timely depart,
      And not returne againe ?
Your sight lends such life to my hart
      That to depart is paine.
Feare yeelds no delay,
      Securenes helpeth pleasure :
Then, till the time gives safer stay,
      O farewell, my live's treasure !

37

The Fairie Queene Prosperina.

Rosseter.   Part I.
(1601).

Harke, al you ladies that do sleep !
　　Thé fayry queen Proserpina
Bids you awake and pitie them that weep.
　　You may doe in the darke
　　　　What the day doth forbid ;
　　Feare not the dogs that barke,
　　　　Night will have all hid.

But if you let your lovers mone,
　　The Fairie Queene Proserpina
Will send abroad her Fairies ev'rie one,
　　That shall pinch blacke and blew
　　　　Your white hands and faire armes
　　That did not kindly rue
　　　　Your Paramours harmes.

In Myrtle Arbours on the downes
　　The Fairie Queene Proserpina,
This night by moone-shine leading merrie
　　rounds,
　　Holds a watch with sweet love,
　　　　Down the dale, up the hill ;
　　No plaints or groanes may move
　　　　Their holy vigill.

38

Campion.

All you that will hold watch with love,
    The Fairie Queene Proserpina
Will make you fairer than Dione's dove
    Roses red, Lillies white,
        And the cleare damaske hue,
    Shall on your cheekes alight :
        Love will adorne you.

All you that love or lov'd before,
    The Fairie Queene Proserpina
Bids you encrease that loving humour more :
    They that yet have not fed
        On delight amorous,
    She vows that they shall lead
        Apes in Avernus.

It fell on a Sommer's Day.

Rosseter's Booke of Ayres. Part I. (1601).

It fell on a sommer's day,
While sweete Bessie sleeping laie,
In her bowre, on her bed,
Light with curtaines shadowed,
Jamy came: shee him spies,
Opning halfe her heavie eies.

Jamy stole in through the dore,
She lay slumb'ring as before;
Softly to her he drew neere,
She heard him, yet would not heare:
Bessie vowed not to speake,
He resolv'd that dumpe to breake.

First a soft kisse he doth take,
She lay still, and would not wake;
Then his hands learn'd to woo,
She dreamp't not what he would doo,
But still slept, while he smild
To see love by sleepe beguild.

Jamy then began to play,
Bessie as one buried lay,
Gladly still through this sleight,
Deceiv'd in her owne deceit;
And since this traunce begoon,
She sleepes ev'rie afternoone.

Maydes are Simple.

Third Booke of Ayres
(1617 ?).

MAYDES are simple, some men say,
They, forsooth, will trust no men.
But should they men's wils obey,
Maides were very simple then.

Truth a rare flower now is growne,
Few men weare it in their hearts ;
Lovers are more easily knowne
By their follies, then deserts.

Safer may we credit give
To a faithlesse wandring Jew
Then a young man's vowes beleeve
When he sweares his love is true.

Love they make a poore blinde childe,
But let none trust such as hee :
Rather then to be beguil'd,
Ever let me simple be.

—◦◦◦—

Think'st Thou to seduce Me then with Words.

Fourth Booke of Ayre,
(1617 ?).

THINK'ST thou to seduce me then with words
    that have no meaning ?
Parrats so can learne to prate, our speech by
    pieces gleaning :
Nurces teach their children so about the time
    of weaning.

Learne to speake first, then to wooe : to wooing,
    much pertayneth :
Hee that courts us, wanting Arte, soone falters
    when he fayneth,
Lookes asquint on his discourse, and smiles,
    when hee complaineth.

Skilfull Anglers hide their hookes, fit baytes for
    every season ;
But with crooked pins fish thou, as babes doe,
    that want reason :
Gogions onely can be caught with such poore
    trickes of treason.

Ruth forgive me, if I err'd from humane heart's
    compassion,
When I laught sometimes too much to see thy
    foolish fashion :
But, alas, who lesse could doe that found so
    good occasion ?

Fain would I Wed.

Fourth Booke of
Ayres (1617?).—A. H. B.

FAIN would I wed a fair young man that day
and night could please me,
When my mind or body grieved that had the
power to ease me.
Maids are full of longing thoughts that breed a
bloodless sickness,
And that, oft I hear men say, is only cured by
quickness.
Oft I have been wooed and prayed, but never
could be moved ;
Many for a day or so I have most dearly loved,
But this foolish mind of mine straight loathes
the thing resolved ;
If to love be sin in me that sin is soon absolved.
Sure I think I shall at last fly to some holy
order ;
When I once am settled there then can I fly no
farther.
Yet I would not die a maid, because I had a
mother ;
As I was by one brought forth I would bring
forth another.

—∿∿∿—

Ev'ry Dame affects good Fame.

Fourth Booke of Ayres (1617?).

Ev'ry dame affects good fame, what ere her
    doings be :
But true prayse is Vertues Bayes which none
    may weare but she.
Borrow'd guise fits not the wise, a simple look
    is best ;
Native grace becomes a face, though ne'er so
    rudely drest.
Now such new found toyes are sold, these
    women to disguise,
That before the yeare growes old the newest
    fashion dyes.

Dames of yore contended more in goodnesse
    to exceede
Then in pride to be envi'd, for that which least
    they neede.
Little Lawne then serv'd the Pawne, if Pawne
    at all there were ;
Homespun thread, and houshold bread, then
    held out all the yeare.
But th' attyres of women now weare out both
    house and land ;
That the wives in silkes may flow, at ebbe the
    Good-men stand.

Once agen, Astrea, then, from heav'n to earth
    descend,
And vouchsafe in their behalfe these errours to
    amend !
Aid from heav'n must make all ev'n, things are
    so out of frame ;
For let man strive all he can, hee needes must
    please his Dame.
Happy man, content that gives and what hee
    gives, enjoys !
Happy dame, content that lives and breakes no
    sleepe for toyes !

—⁓ΛΛΛ⁓—

Thou joy'st, Fond Boy.

Fourth   Booke   of
Ayres (1617 ?).

Thou joy'st, fond boy, to be by many loved,
To have thy beauty of most dames approved ;
For this dost thou thy native worth disguise
And play'st the Sycophant t' observe their eyes ;
Thy glasse thou councel'st more t' adorne thy
    skin,
That first should schoole thee to be fayre
    within.

'Tis childish to be caught with Pearle or
    Amber,
And woman-like too much to cloy the chamber ;
Youths should the Field affect, heate their
    rough Steedes,
Their hardned nerves to fit for better deedes.

Is't not more joy strong Holds to force with
    swords,
Then women's weaknesse take with lookes or
    words?

Men that doe noble things all purchase glory :
One man for one brave Act hath prov'd a
    story :
But if that one tenne thousand Dames o'er-
    came,
Who would record it, if not to his shame?
'Tis farre more conquest with one to live true,
Than every hour to triumph Lord of new.

—⁓⌇⁓—

Silly Boy, 'tis full Moon yet.   Third Booke of Ayres (1617 ?).

SILLY boy, 'tis ful moone yet, thy night as day
    shines clearely ;
Had thy youth but wit to feare, thou couldst not
    love so dearely.
Shortly wilt thou mourne when all thy pleasures
    are bereaved ;
Little knowes he how to love that never was
    deceived.

This is thy first mayden flame, that triumphes
    yet unstayned ;
All is artlesse now you speake, not one word yet
    is fayned ;

Campion.

All is heav'n that you behold, and all your
  thoughts are blessed ;
But no spring can want his fall, each Troylus
  hath his Cresseid.

Thy well-order'd lockes ere long shall rudely
  hang neglected ;
And thy lively pleasant cheare reade griefe on
  earth dejected.
Much then wilt thou blame thy Saint, that
  made thy heart so holy,
And with sighes confesse, in love, that too much
  faith is folly.

Yet be just and constant still !   Love may
  beget a wonder,
Not unlike a summer's frost, or winter's fatall
  thunder.
Hee that holds his sweethart true, unto his day
  of dying,
Lives, of all that ever breath'd, most worthy
  the envÿing.

If Thou longest.
Third Booke of Ayres (1617?).

IF thou longest so much to learne, sweet boy,
    what 'tis to love,
Doe but fix thy thought on mee and thou shalt
    quickly prove.
        Little suit, at first, shall win
            Way to thy abasht desire,
        But then will I hedge thee in
            Salamander-like with fire.

With thee dance I will, and sing, and thy fond
    dalliance beare ;
We the grovy hils will climbe, and play the
    wantons there ;
        Other whiles wee'le gather flowres,
            Lying dalying on the grasse !
        And thus our delightful howres
            Full of waking dreames shall passe !

When thy joyes were thus at height, my love
    should turne from thee ;
Old acquaintance then should grow as strange
    as strange might be ;
        'Twenty rivals thou shouldst finde,
            Breaking all their hearts for mee,
        While to all I'le prove more kinde
            And more forward then to thee.

Thus, thy silly youth, enrag'd, would soone my
    love defie ;
But, alas, poore soule too late ! clipt wings can
    never flye.
      Those sweet houres which wee had past,
          Cal'd to minde, thy heart would
          burne ;
      And couldst thou flye ne'er so fast,
          They would make thee straight
          returne.

—⁄⋀⋁⋁—

Break now, my Heart.

Third Booke of Ayres
(1617 ?).

BREAKE now, my heart, and dye ! O no, she
    may relent.
Let my despaire prevayle ! Oh stay, hope is not
    spent.
Should she now fixe one smile on thee, where
    were despair ?
  The losse is but easie, which smiles can repayre.
  A stranger would please thee, if she were as
    fayre.

Her must I love or none, so sweet none breathes
    as shee ;
The more is my despayre, alas, shee loves not
    mee !
But cannot time make way for love through
    ribs of steele ?
  The Grecian inchanted all parts but the heele,
  At last a shaft daunted, which his hart did feele.

The Peacefull Westerne Winde.

Light Conceits of Lovers (1613?).

THE peacefull westerne winde
The winter stormes hath tam'd,
And nature in each kinde
The kinde heat hath inflam'd :
The forward buds so sweetly breathe
Out of their earthy bowers,
That heav'n which viewes their pompe beneath,
Would faine be deckt with flowers.

See how the morning smiles
On her bright easterne hill,
And with soft steps beguiles
Them that lie slumbring still !
The musicke-loving birds are come
From cliffes and rockes unknowne,
To see the trees and briers blome
That late were overflowne.

What Saturn did destroy,
Love's Queene revives againe ;
And now her naked boy
Doth in the fields remaine,
Where he such pleasing change doth view
In every living thing,
As if the world were borne anew
To gratifie the Spring.

Campion.

If all things life present,
Why die my comforts then?
Why suffers my content?
Am I the worst of men?
O beautie, be not thou accus'd
Too justly in this case!
Unkindly if true love be us'd,
'Twill yeeld thee little grace.

—/\/\/\/·—

There is None.

Light   Conceits   of
Lovers (1613?).

THERE is none, O none but you,
That from mee estrange your sight,
Whom mine eyes affect to view
Or chained eares heare with delight.

Other beauties others move,
In you I all graces finde;
Such is the effect of love,
To make them happy that are kinde.

Women in fraile beauty trust,
Onely seeme you faire to mee;
Yet prove truely kinde and just,
For that may not dissembled be.

Sweet, afford mee then your sight,
That, survaying all your lookes,
Endlesse volumes I may write
And fill the world with envyed bookes:

Which when after-ages view,
    All shall wonder and despaire,
Woman to find man so true,
    Or man a woman half so faire.

—∿∿∿—

Sweet, exclude Mee not.

Light Conceits of Lovers (1613?).

Sweet, exclude mee not, nor be divided
    From him that ere long must bed thee :
All thy maiden doubts law hath decided ;
    Sure wee are, and I must wed thee.
Presume then yet a little more :
Here's the way, barre not the dore.

Tenants, to fulfill their Landlord's pleasure,
    Pay their rent before the quarter :
'Tis my case, if you it rightly measure ;
    Put mee not then off with laughter.
Consider then a little more :
Here's the way to all my store.

Why were dores in love's despight devised ?
    Are not Lawes enough restrayning ?
Women are most apt to be surprised
    Sleeping, or sleepe wisely fayning.
Then grace me yet a little more :
Here's the way, barre not the dore.

Campion.

Now hath Flora.

Song from the " Masque at the Marriage of the Lord Hayes," 1606.
"As soon as they came to the descent toward the dancing place, the concert of ten ceased, and the four Sylvans played the same air, to which Zephyrus and the two other Sylvans did sing these words in a bass, tenor, and treble voice, and going up and down as they sung they strewed flowers all about the place."—A. H, B.

Now hath Flora rob'd her bowers
To befrend this place with flowers :
    Strowe aboute, strowe aboute !
The Skye rayn'd never kindlyer showers.
Flowers with Bridalls well agree,
Fresh as brides and bridgroomes be :
    Strowe aboute, strowe aboute !
And mixe them with fit melodie.
    Earth hath no Princelier flowers
Then Roses white and Roses red,
But they must still be mingled :
And as a rose new pluckt from Venus' thorn,
So doth a bride her bridegroome's bed adorne.

Divers divers flowers affect
For some private deare respect :
    Strowe aboute, strowe aboute !
Let every one his owne protecte ;
But he's none of Flora's friend
That will not the Rose commend.
    Strowe aboute, strowe aboute !

Lyric Poems.

Let Princes Princely flowers defend :
    Roses, the garden's pride,
Are flowers for love and flowers for Kinges,
In courts desired, aud Weddings :
And as a rose in Venus' bosome worne,
So doth a Bridegroome his Bride's bed adorne.

—ᴧᴧᴧᴧ—

Her Rosie Cheekes.

Light Conceits of Lovers (1613 ?). 'Currall' (l. 5), Coral.

Her rosie cheekes, her ever smiling eyes,
Are Spheares and beds, where Love in triumph
    lies :
Her rubine lips, when they their pearle unlocke,
Make them seeme as they did rise
All out of one smooth Currall Rocke.
Oh that of other Creatures' store I knew
More worthy and more rare :
For these are old, and shee so new,
That her to them none should compare.

O could she love, would shee but heare a friend ;
Or that shee onely knew what sighs pretend.
Her lookes inflame, yet cold as Ice is she.
Doe or speake, all's to one end,
For what shee is that will shee be.
Yet will I never cease her prayse to sing,
Though she gives no regard :
For they that grace a worthlesse thing,
Are onely greedy of reward.

Campion.

Come Away.
Light   Conceits   of
Lovers (1613 ?).

Come away, arm'd with love's delights,
 Thy sprightfull graces bring with thee,
When love's longing fights,
 They must the sticklers be.
Come quickly, come, the promis'd houre is
 wel-nye spent,
And pleasure being too much deferr'd, looseth
 her best content.

Is shee come? O, how neare is shee?
 How farre yet from this friendly place?
How many steps from me?
 When shall I her imbrace?
These armes I'le spred, which onely at her
 sight shall close,
Attending as the starry flowre that the Sun's
 noonetide knowes.

—∿∿∿—

What Harvest.
Light   Conceits   of
Lovers (1613 ?).

What harvest halfe so sweet is
As still to reape the kisses
 Growne ripe in sowing?
And straight to be receiver
Of that which thou art giver,
 Rich in bestowing?

55

Kisse then, my harvest Queene,
    Full garners heaping ;
Kisses, ripest when th' are greene,
    Want onely reaping.

The Dove alone expresses
Her fervencie in kisses,
    Of all most loving :
A creature as offencelesse
As those things that are sencelesse
    And void of moving.
Let us so love and kisse,
    Though all envie us :
That which kinde, and harmlesse is,
    None can denie us.

--ᐱᐯ--

So many Loves. Light Conceits of Lovers (1613?).

So many loves have I neglected,
    Whose good parts might move mee,
That now I live of all rejected,
    There is none will love me.
Why is mayden heat so coy?
    It freezeth when it burneth,
Looseth what it might injoy,
    And, having lost it, mourneth.

Should I then wooe, that have beene wooed,
    Seeking them that flye mee?
When I my faith with teares have vowed,
    And when all denye mee,

Campion.

Who will pitty my disgrace,
  Which love might have prevented?
There is no submission base
  Where error is repented.

O happy men, whose hopes are licenc'd
  To discourse their passion,
While women are confin'd to silence,
  Loosing wisht occasion!
Yet our tongues then theirs, men say,
  Are apter to be moving:
Women are more dumbe then they,
  But in their thoughts more moving.

When I compare my former strangenesse
  With my present doting,
I pitty men that speak in plainnesse,
  Their true heart's devoting;
While we with repentance jest
  At their submissive passion.
Maydes, I see, are never blest,
  That strange be but for fashion.

—⋏⋀⋀⋏—

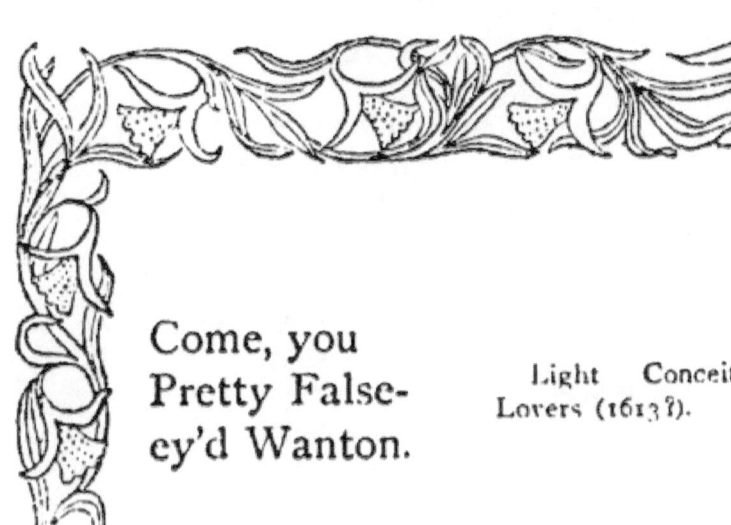

Come, you Pretty False-ey'd Wanton.

Light Conceits of Lovers (1613?).

Come, you pretty false-ey'd wanton,
  Leave your crafty smiling!
Think you to escape me now
  With slipp'ry words beguiling!
No; you mockt me th'other day;
  When you got loose, you fled away;
But, since I have caught you now,
  I'le clip your wings for flying:
Smoth'ring kisses fast I'le heape,
  And keepe you so from crying.

Sooner may you count the starres,
  And number hayle downe pouring,
Tell the osiers of the Temmes,
  Or Goodwin's Sands devouring,
Then the thicke-shower'd kisses here
  Which now thy tyred lips must beare.
Such a harvest never was,
  So rich and full of pleasure,
But 'tis spent as soone as reapt,
  So trustlesse is love's treasure.

Campion.

Would it were dumb midnight now,
   When all the world lyes sleeping !
Would this place some Desert were,
   Which no man hath in keeping !
My desires should then be safe,
   And when you cry'd then would I laugh :
But if aught might breed offence,
   Love onely should be blamed :
I would live your servant still,
   And you my Saint unnamed.

—∿∿∿—

Where shall I Refuge Seek.

Light Conceits of Lovers (1613 ?).

Where shall I refuge seek, if you refuse mee ?
In you my hope, in you my fortune lyes,
In you my life, though you unjust accuse me,
My service scorne, and merit underprise :
    Oh bitter griefe ! that exile is become
    Reward for faith, and pittie deafe and dumbe.

Why should my firmnesse finde a seate so
      wav'ring ?
My simple vowes, my love you entertain'd ;
Without desert the same againe disfav'ring ;
Yet I my word and passion hold unstain'd.
    O wretched me ! that my chiefe joy should
      breede
    My onely griefe, and kindnesse pitty neede.

Lyric Poems.

The Sypres Curten.

Rosseter. Part I.
(1601). 'Sypres' (l. 1),
cypress.

The Sypres curten of the night is spread,
And over all a silent dewe is cast.
The weaker cares by sleepe are conquered :
But I alone, with hidious grief agast,
In spite of Morpheus charmes, a watch doe
keepe
Over mine eies, to banish carelesse sleepe.

Yet oft my trembling eyes through faintnes
close,
And then the Mappe of hell before me stands,
Which Ghosts doe see, and I am one of those
Ordain'd to pine in sorrowes endles bands,
Since from my wretched soule all hopes are reft,
And now no cause of life to me is left.

Griefe ceaze my soul, for that will still endure
When my cras'd body is consum'd and gone ;
Beare it to thy blacke denne, there keepe it sure
Where thou ten thousand soules doest tyre
upon !
Yet all doe not affoord such foode to thee
As this poore one, the worser part of mee.

—ᴧᴧ—

Tell me, Gentle Howre of Night.

Song of two Voices, a bass and tenor, sung by a Sylvan and an Hour at the " Masque at the Marriage of the Lord Hayes." Twelfth Night (1606).

SILVAN.

Tell me, gentle howre of night,
Wherein dost thou most delight?

HOWRE.

Not in sleepe.

SILVAN.

Wherein then?

HOWRE.

In the frolicke vew of men?

SILVAN.

Lovest thou Musicke?

HOWRE.

O 'tis sweet

SILVAN.

What's dauncing?

HOWRE.

Ev'n the mirth of feete

SILVAN.

Joy you in Fayries and in elves

Lyric Poems.

HOWRE.

We are of that sort ourselves.
But, Silvan, say why do you love
Onely to frequent the grove?

SILVAN.

Life is fullest of content,
Where delight is innocent.

HOWRE.

Pleasure must varie, not be long.
Come then let's close, and end our song.

CHORUS.

Yet, ere we vanish from this princely sight,
Let us bid Phœbus and his states good-night.

Night as well as Brightest Day.

A song of three voices with divers instruments. From the Masque given by Lord Knowles to Queen Anne : at Cawsome House, near Reading. April, 1613. "At the end of this song enters Sylvanus, shaped after the description of the ancient writers ; his lower parts like a goat, and his upper parts in an antic habit of rich taffeta, cut into leaves, and on his head he had a false hair, with a wreath of long boughs and lilies, that hung dangling about his neck, and in his hand a cypress branch, in memory of his love Cyparissus."

Night as well as brightest day hath her delight,
Let us then with mirth and Musicke decke the
    night.
Never did glad day such store
  Of joy to night bequeath :
Her Starres then adore,
    Both in Heav'n, and here beneath.

Love and beautie, mirth and musicke yeeld true
    joyes,
Though the Cynickes in their folly count them
    toyes.
Raise your spirits ne're so high,
  They will be apt to fall :
None brave thoughts envie,
    Who had ere brave thought at all.

Joy is the sweete friend of life, the nurse of
　　blood,
Patron of all health, and fountaine of all good:
Never may joy hence depart,
　　But all your thoughts attend ;
Nought can hurt the heart,
　　That retaines so sweete a friend.

—◊◊◊—

Follow your Saint.

Rosseter's　Booke　of
Ayres.　Part I.　(1601).

FOLLOW your Saint, follow with accents
　　sweet !
Haste you, sad noates, fall at her flying fleete !
There, wrapt in cloud of sorrowe, pitie move,
And tell the ravisher of my soule, I perish for
　　her love :
But if she scorns my never-ceasing paine,
Then burst with sighing in her sight and ne're
　　returne againe !

All that I soong still to her praise did tend ;
Still she was first, still she my songs did end,
Yet she my love and Musicke both doth flie,
The Musicke that her Eccho is and beauties
　　sympathie.
Then let my Noates pursue her scornefull flight !
It shall suffice, that they were breath'd, and dyed
　　for her delight.

Faire, if you Expect.

A Booke of Ayres (1601).

Faire, if you expect admiring,
Sweet, if you provoke desiring,
Grace deere love with kind requiting.
Fond, but if thy sight be blindnes,
False, if thou affect unkindnes,
Flie both love and love's delighting !
Then when hope is lost and love is scorned,
Ile bury my desires, and quench the fires that
     ever yet in vaine have burned.

Fates, if you rule lovers' fortune,
Stars, if men your powers importune,
Yield reliefe by your relenting ;
Time, if sorrow be not endles,
Hope made vaine, and pittie friendles,
Helpe to ease my long lamenting.
But if griefes remaine still unredressed,
I'le flie to her againe, and sue for pitie to renue
     my hopes distressed.

Blame not My Cheeks.

A Booke of Ayres.

Blame not my cheeks, though pale with love
    they be ;
The kindly heate unto my heart is flowne,
To cherish it that is dismaid by thee,

Who art so cruell and unsteedfast growne :
For Nature, cald for by distressed harts,
Neglects and quite forsakes the outward partes.

But they whose cheekes with careles blood are
    stain'd,
Nurse not one sparke of love within their harts ;
And, when they woe, they speake with passion
    fain'd,
For their fat love lyes in their outward parts :
But in their brests, where love his court should
    hold,
Poore Cupid sits, and blowes his nailes for cold.

—◦◦◦—

When the God of Merrie Love.

A Booke of Ayres (1601).

When the god of merrie love
As yet in his cradle lay,
Thus his wither'd nurse did say :
"Thou a wanton boy wilt prove
To deceive the powers above ;
For by thy continuall smiling
I see thy power of beguiling."

Therewith she the babe did kisse ;
When a sodaine fire outcame
From those burning lips of his,
That did her with love enflame.
But none would regard the same :
So that, to her daie of dying,
The old wretch liv'd ever crying.

Campion.

Woo Her, and Win Her.

Song from the Lord's Masque, presented in the Banqueting House on the Marriage Night of the High and Mighty Count Palatine, and the Royally descended the Lady Elizabeth. (Shrove-Sunday 1612-1613).

Woo her, and win her, he that can;
  Each woman hath two lovers,
So she must take and leave a man,
  Till time more grace discovers.
This doth Jove to shew that want
  Makes beauty most respected;
If fair women were more scant,
  They would be more affected.

Courtship and music suit with love,
  They both are works of passion;
Happy is he whose words can move,
  Yet sweet notes help persuasion.
Mix your words with music then,
  That they the more may enter;
Bold assaults are fit for men,
  That on strange beauties venture.

Lyric Poems.

Jacke and Jone They thinke no Ill.

Divine and Morall Songs.

J ACKE and Jone they thinke no ill,
But loving live, and merry still ;
Do their weeke-dayes' worke, and pray
Devotely on the holy day :
Skip and trip it on the greene,
And help to chuse the Summer Queene ;
Lash out, at a Country Feast,
Their silver penny with the best.

Well can they judge of nappy Ale,
And tell at large a Winter tale ;
Climbe up to the Apple loft,
And turne the crabs till they be soft.
Tib is all the father's joy,
And little Tom the mother's boy.
All their pleasure is Content ;
And care, to pay their yearely rent.

Jone can call by name her Cowes,
And decke her windowes with greene boughs ;
Shee can wreathes and tuttyes make,
And trimme with plums a Bridall Cake.
Jacke knowes what brings gaine or losse ;
And his long Flaile can stoutly tosse,
Make the hedge which others break,
And ever thinkes what he doth speake.

68

Campion.

Now you Courtly Dames and Knights,
That study onely strange delights ;
Though you scorn the homespun gray,
And revell in your rich array :
Though your tongues dissemble deepe,
And can your heads from danger keepe ;
Yet for all your pomp and traine,
Securer lives the silly Swaine.

—◠◠◠—

Come Ashore, Come.

Songs from the " Masque at the Marriage of the Earl of Somerset and the Lady Francis Howard," Saint Stephen's Night, 1613.

"Straight in the Thames appeared four barges with skippers in them, and withall this song was sung."

"At the conclusion of this [first] song arrived twelve skippers in red caps, with short cassocks and long flaps wide at the knees. of white canvas striped with crimson, white gloves and pumps, and red stockings : these twelve danced a brave and lively dance, shouting and triumphing after their manner."

I.

Come ashore, come, merry mates,
With your nimble heels and pates :
Summon ev'ry man his knight,
Enough honoured is this night.
Now, let your sea-born goddess come,
Quench these lights, and make all dumb.
Some sleep ; others let her call :
And so good-night to all, good-night to all.

II.

Haste aboard, haste now away !
Hymen frowns at your delay.
Hymen doth long nights affect ;
Yield him then his due respect.
The sea-born goddess straight will come,
Quench these lights, and make all dumb.
Some sleep ; others she will call :
And so good-night to all, good-night to all.

—⋀⋁⋀⋁⋀—

Of Neptune's Empire.

"Written in 1594," says Mr Bullen, for the Gray's Inn Masque *Gesta Graiorum*, "which is printed in Nichols' *Progresses of Queen Elizabeth*."

Of Neptune's Empire let us sing,
At whose command the waves obey ;
To whom the rivers tribute pay,
Down the high mountains sliding :
To whom the scaly nation yields
Homage for the crystal fields
    Wherein they dwell :
And every sea-god pays a gem
Yearly out of his wat'ry cell
To deck great Neptune's diadem.

The Tritons dancing in a ring
Before his palace gates do make
The water with their echoes quake,
Like the great thunder sounding :

Campion.

The sea-nymphs chant their accents shrill
And the sirens, taught to kill
   With their sweet voice,
Make ev'ry echoing rock reply
Unto their gentle murmuring noise
The praise of Neptune's empery.

—∿∿∿—

Shall I Come.

A Booke of Ayres.
Part II. (1601).

SHAL I come, if I swim? wide are ye waves,
   you see :
Shall I come, if I flie, my deere Love, to thee?
Streames Venus will appease ; Cupid gives me
   winges ;
All the powers assist my desire
Save you alone, that set my wofull heart on
   fire !

You are faire, so was Hero that in Sestos dwelt ;
She a priest, yet the heat of love truly felt.
A greater streame then this, did her love de-
   vide ;
But she was his guide with a light :
So through the streames Leander did enjoy
   her sight.

—∿∿∿—

Oft have I Sigh'd.

The First Song in the Third Booke of Ayres (1617 ?).

OFT have I sigh'd for him that heares me
   not;
Who absent hath both love and mee forgot.
O yet I languish still through his delay:
Dayes seeme as yeares when wisht friends breake
   their day.

Had he but lov'd as common lovers use,
His faithlesse stay some kindnesse would ex-
   cuse:
O yet I languish still, still constant mourne
For him that can breake vowes, but not returne.

72

Campion.

Now let her
Change.

The Second Song in
the Third Booke of
Ayres (1617 ?).

Now let her change and spare not !
Since she proves strange I care not :
 Fain'd love charm'd so my delight,
That still I doted on her sight.
But she is gone, new joyes imbracing
And my desires disgracing.

When did I erre in blindnesse,
Or vexe her with unkindnesse?
If my cares serv'd her alone,
Why is shee thus untimely gone?
True love abides to t' houre of dying :
False love is ever flying.

False, then farewell for ever !
Once false proves faithfull never :
He that boasts now of thy love,
Shall soone my present fortunes prove.
Were he as faire as bright Adonis,
Faith is not had, where none is.

—✲✲✲—

Were my Hart. Third Booke of Ayres (1617?).

Were my hart as some men's are, thy
    errours would not move me ;
But thy faults I curious finde and speake be-
    cause I love thee :
Patience is a thing divine and farre, I grant,
    above mee.

Foes sometimes befriend us more, our blacker
    deedes objecting,
Then th' obsequious bosome guest, with false
    respect affecting.
Friendship is the Glasse of Truth, our hidden
    staines detecting.

While I use of eyes enjoy and inward light of
    reason,
Thy observer will I be and censor, but in
    season :
Hidden mischiefe to conceale in State and
    Love is treason.

—⁓∿∿⁓—

So Tyr'd. Third Booke of Ayres (1617?).

So tyr'd are all my thoughts, that sence and
    spirits faile :
Mourning I pine, and know not what I ayle.
O what can yeeld ease to a minde
        Joy in nothing that can finde ?

Campion.

How are my powres fore-spoke? What strange
    distaste is this?
Hence, cruell hate of that which sweetest is!
Come, come delight! make my dull braine
        Feele once heate of joy againe.

The lover's teares are sweet, their mover makes
    them so;
Proud of a wound the bleeding souldiers grow.
Poor I alone, dreaming, endure
      Grief that knowes nor cause, nor cure.

And whence can all this grow? even from an
    idle minde,
That no delight in any good can finde.
Action alone makes the soule blest:
        Vertue dyes with too much rest.

—ᴧᴧᴧ—

Why Presumes Thy Pride.

Third Booke of Ayres (1617?).

Why presumes thy pride on that that must
    so private be,
Scarce that it can good be cal'd, tho' it
    seemes best to thee,
Best of all that Nature fram'd or curious eye
    can see.

'Tis thy beauty, foolish Maid, that like a
　　blossome, growes;
Which who viewes no more enjoyes than on a
　　bush a rose,
That, by manie's handling, fades: and thou
　　art one of those.

If to one thou shalt prove true and all beside
　　reject,
Then art thou but one man's good; which
　　yeelds a poore effect:
For the common'st good by farre deserves the
　　best respect.

But if for this goodnesse thou thyself wilt
　　common make,
Thou art then not good at all: so thou canst
　　no way take
But to prove the meanest good or else all good
　　forsake.

Be not then of beauty proud, but so her colours
　　beare
That they prove not staines to her, that them
　　for grace should weare:
So shalt thou to all more fayre then thou wert
　　born appeare.

—◠◡◠—

Campion.

O Griefe, O Spite.

Third Booke of Ayres (1617 ?).

O GRIEFE, O spite, to see poore Vertue
scorn'd,
Truth far exil'd, False Arte lov'd, Vice ador'd,
Free Justice sold, worst causes best adorn'd,
Right cast by Powre, Pittie in vaine implor'd !
O who in such an age could wish to live,
When none can have or hold, but such as give ?

O times ! O men ! to Nature rebels growne,
Poore in desert, in name rich, proud of shame,
Wise but in ill ! Your stiles are not your owne,
Though dearely bought, honour is honest
fame.
Old Stories only, goodnesse now containe,
And the true wisedome that is just and plaine.

—◇◇◇—

O Never to be Moved.

Third Booke of Ayres (1617 ?).

O NEVER to be moved,
O beauty unrelenting !
Hard hart, too dearely loved !
Fond love, too late repenting !

Why did I dreame of too much blisse?
Deceitfull hope was cause of this,
   O heare me speake this, and no more,
    Live you in joy, while I my woes deplore!

   All comforts despayred
    Distaste your bitter scorning;
Great sorrowes unrepayred
   Admit no meane in mourning:
Dye, wretch, since hope from thee is fled.
He that must dye is better dead.
   O deare delight, yet ere I dye,
    Some pitty shew, though you reliefe deny!

—⌇⌇⌇—

Good Wife.

Third Booke of Ayres
(1617?).—A. H. B.

WHAT is it all that men possess, among themselves conversing?
Wealth or fame, or some such boast, scarce
   worthy the rehearsing.
Women only are men's good, with them in
   love conversing.

If weary, they prepare us rest; if sick, their
   hand attends us;
When with grief our hearts are prest, their
   comfort best befriends us:
Sweet or sour, they willing go to share what
   fortune sends us.

Campion.

What pretty babes with pain they bear, our
    name and form presenting !
What we get, how wise they keep ! by sparing,
    wants preventing ;
Sorting all their household cares to our observed
    contenting.

All this, of whose large use I sing, in two words
    is expressed :
Good Wife is the good I praise, if by good
    men possessed ;
Bad with bad in ill suit well ; but good with
    good live blessed.

—⁓⋀⋁⋀⋁⁓—

Fire that must Flame.

Third Booke of Ayres
(1617 ?).--A. H. B.

Fire that must flame is with apt fuel fed,
Flowers that will thrive in sunny soil are bred.
How can a heart feel heat that no hope finds ?
Or can he love on whom no comfort shines ?

Fair ! I confess there's pleasure in your sight !
Sweet ! you have power, I grant, of all delight !
But what is all to me, if I have none ?
Churl, that you are, t'enjoy such wealth alone !

Prayers move the heavens but find no grace
    with you ;
Yet in your looks a heavenly form I view,
Then will I pray again, hoping to find,
As well as in your looks, heaven in your mind !

Lyric Poems.

Saint of my heart, Queen of my life and love,
O let my vows thy loving spirit move!
Let me no longer mourn through thy disdain;
But with one touch of grace cure all my pain.

—∿∿∿—

Thrice Toss these Oaken Ashes.

Third Booke of Ayres
(1617?).—A. H. B.

THRICE toss these oaken ashes in the air,
Thrice sit thou mute in this enchanted chair;
And thrice three times, tie up this true love's
    knot!
And murmur soft "She will, or she will not."

Go burn these poisonous weeds in yon blue
    fire,
These screech-owl's feathers and this prickling
    briar;
This cypress gathered at a dead man's grave;
That all thy fears and cares, an end may have.

Then come, you Fairies, dance with me a
    round!
Melt her hard heart with your melodious sound!
In vain are all the charms I can devise:
She hath an art to break them with her eyes.

Be Thou then my Beauty Named.

Third Booke of Ayres (1617?).—A. H. B.

Be thou then my Beauty named,
  Since thy will is to be mine !
For by that I am enflamed,
  Which on all alike doth shine.
Others may the light admire,
I only truly feel the fire.

But if lofty titles move thee,
  Challenge then a Sovereign's place !
Say I honour when I love thee;
  Let me call thy kindness Grace.
State and Love things diverse be,
Yet will we teach them to agree !

Or if this be not sufficing ;
  Be thou styled my Goddess then :
I will love thee, sacrificing ;
  In thine honour, hymns I'll pen.
To be thine what canst thou more ?
I'll love thee, serve thee, and adore.

—⁓ΛΛ⁓—

Fire, Fire, Fire, Fire!

Third Booke of Ayres
(1617?).—A. H. B.

Fire, fire, fire, fire!
Lo here I burn in such desire
That all the tears that I can strain
Out of mine idle empty brain
Cannot allay my scorching pain.
Come Trent, and Humber, and fair Thames!
Dread Ocean, haste with all thy streams!
    And if you cannot quench my fire,
    O drown both me and my desire!

    Fire, fire, fire, fire!
There is no hell to my desire.
See, all the rivers backward fly!
And th' Ocean doth his waves deny,
For fear my heat should drink them dry!
Come, heavenly showers, then, pouring down!
Come you, that once the world did drown!
Some then you spared, but now save all,
That else must burn, and with me fall!

—✶✶✶—

O Sweet Delight.

Third Booke of Ayres
(1617?).—A. H. B.

O SWEET delight, O more than human bliss,
With her to live that ever loving is ;
To hear her speak, whose words are so well
    placed,
That she by them, as they in her are graced :
Those looks to view, that feast the viewer's eye,
How blest is he that may so live and die !

Such love as this the golden times did know,
When all did reap, yet none took care to sow ;
Such love as this an endless summer makes,
And all distaste from frail affection takes.
So loved, so blessed, in my beloved am I ;
Which till their eyes ache, let iron men envy !

—www—

Thus I Resolve.

Third Booke of Ayres
(1617?).—A. H. B.

THUS I resolve, and time hath taught me so ;
    Since she is fair and ever kind to me,
Though she be wild and wanton-like in show,
    Those little stains in youth I will not see.
That she be constant, heaven I oft implore :
If prayers prevail not, I can do no more.

Palm tree the more you press, the more it
    grows ;
  Leave it alone, it will not much exceed.
Free beauty if you strive to yoke, you lose :
  And for affection, strange distaste you breed.
What Nature hath not taught, no Art can
    frame :
Wild born be wild still, though by force you
    tame.

—ᐱᐱᐱ—

Come, O Come.

Third Booke of Ayres
(1617?).—A. H. B.

Come, O come, my life's delight,
  Let me not in languor pine !
Love loves no delay ; thy sight,
  The more enjoyed, the more divine :
O come, and take from me
The pain of being deprived of thee !

Thou all sweetness dost enclose,
  Like a little world of bliss.
Beauty guards thy looks : the rose
  In them pure and eternal is.
Come, then, and make thy flight
As swift to me, as heavenly light.

Could My Heart.

Third Booke of Ayres
(1617?).—A. H. B.

Could my heart more tongues employ
    Than it harbours thoughts of grief ;
It is now so far from joy,
    That it scarce could ask relief.
Truest hearts by deeds unkind
To despair are most inclined.

Happy minds, that can redeem
    Their engagements how they please !
That no joys or hopes esteem,
    Half so precious as their ease !
Wisdom should prepare men so
As if they did all foreknow.

Yet no art or caution can
    Grown affections easily change ;
Use is such a Lord of man
    That he brooks worst what is strange.
Better never to be blest
Than to lose all at the best.

—⁓∿∿⁓—

Shall I then Hope.

Third Booke of Ayres
(1617?).—A. H. B.

Shall I then hope when faith is fled ?
Can I seek love when hope is gone ?
    Or can I live when love is dead ?
Poorly he lives, that can love none.

Her vows are broke and I am free ;
She lost her faith in losing me.

When I compare mine own events,
When I weigh others' like annoy ;
All do but heap up discontents
That on a beauty build their joy.
Thus I of all complain, since she
All faith hath lost in losing me.

So my dear freedom have I gained,
Through her unkindness and disgrace :
Yet could I ever live enchained,
As she my service did embrace.
But she is changed, and I am free :
Faith failing her, love died in me.

—ᴡᴡ—

Leave Pro-longing.

Fourth Booke of Ayres
(1617 ?).

Leave prolonging thy distresse !
All delayes afflict the dying.
Many lost sighes long I spent, to her for mercy
crying ;
But now, vain mourning, cease !
I'll dye, and mine owne griefes release.

Thus departing from this light
To those shades that end all sorrow,
Yet a small time of complaint, a little breath
Ile borrow,
To tell my once delight
I dye alone through her despight.

Respect My Faith.

Fourth Booke of Ayres (1617?).

RESPECT my faith, regard my service past ;
The hope you wing'd call home to you at last.
Great prise it is that I in you shall gaine,
So great for you hath been my losse and paine.
   My wits I spent and time for you alone,
     Observing you and losing all for one.

Some rais'd to rich estates in this time are,
That held their hopes to mine inferiour farre :
Such, scoffing mee, or pittying me, say thus,
" Had hee not loved, he might have liv'd
     like us."
   O, then, deare sweet, for love and pitties
     sake
   My faith reward, and from me scandall
     take.

—◦◦◦—

Vaile, Love, Mine Eyes !

Fourth Booke of Ayres (1617?).

VAILE, Love, mine eyes !   O hide from me
   The plagues that charge the curious minde !
If beauty private will not be,
   Suffice it yet that she proves kinde,
Who can usurp heav'ns light alone.
Stars were not made to shine on one.

Griefs past recure fooles try to heale,
   That greater harmes on lesse inflict,
The pure offend by too much zeale ;
   Affection should not be too strict.
Hee that a true embrace will finde,
To beauties faults must still be blinde.

—ᴧᴧᴧᴧ—

Love Me or Not.

Fourth Booke of Ayres
(1617 ?).

LOVE me or not, love her I must or dye ;
Leave me or not, follow her, needs must I.
O that her grace would my wisht comforts give !
How rich in her, how happy should I live !

All my desire, all my delight should be,
Her to enjoy, her to unite to mee :
Envy should cease, her would I love alone :
Who loves by lookes, is seldome true to one.

Could I enchant, and that it lawfull were,
Her would I charme softly that none should
    heare.
But love enforc'd rarely yeelds firme content ;
So would I love that neyther should repent.

—ᴧᴧᴧᴧ—

What Meanes this Folly.

Fourth Booke of Ayres (1617 ?).

Wнат meanes this folly, now to brave it so,
　　And then to use submission?
Is that a friend that straight can play the foe?
　　Who loves on such condition?

Though Bryars breede Roses, none the Bryar
　　　　affect;
　　But with the flowre are pleased.
Love onely loves delight and soft respect:
　　He must not be diseased.

These thorny passions spring from barren
　　　　breasts,
　　Or such as neede much weeding.
Love onely loves delight and soft respect,
　　But sends them not home bleeding.

Command thy humour, strive to give content,
　　And shame not love's profession.
Of kindnesse never any could repent
　　That made choyce with discretion.

—∿∿—

Deare, if I with Guile.

Fourth Booke of Ayres
(1617 ?).

DEARE, if I with guile would guild a true
  intent,
Heaping flattries that in heart were never
    meant :
        Easely could I then obtaine
          What now in vaine I force ;
        Falshood much doth gaine,
          Truth yet holds the better course.

Love forbid that through dissembling I should
    thrive,
Or in praysing you, myselfe of truth deprive !
        Let not your high thoughts debase
          A simple truth in me :
        Great is beauties grace,
          Truth is yet as fayre as she !

Prayse is but the winde of pride, if it exceedes ;
Wealth, pris'd in itselfe, no outward value
    needes.
        Fayre you are, and passing fayre ;
          You know it, and 'tis true :
        Yet let none despayre
          But to finde as fayre as you.

—◠◠◠◠—

O Love, where are thy Shafts.

Fourth Booke of Ayres (1617?).

O LOVE, where are thy Shafts, thy Quiver,
    and thy Bow?
Shall my wounds onely weepe, and he ungaged
    goe?
Be just, and strike him to, that dares con-
    temne thee so!

No eyes are like to thine, though men suppose
    thee blinde;
So fayre they levell when the marke they list
    to finde:
Then, strike, O strike the heart that beares
    the cruell minde!

Is my fond sight deceived? or doe I Cupid spye,
Close ayming at his breast, by whom despis'd,
    I dye?
Shoot home, sweet Love, and wound him,
    that hee may not flye!

O then we both will sit in some unhaunted
    shade,
And heale each other's wound which Love
    hath justly made:
O hope, O thought too vaine! how quickly
    dost thou fade!

At large he wanders still: his heart is free
   from paine ;
While secret sighes I spend, and teares, but
   all in vaine.
Yet, Love, thou know'st, by right, I should
   not thus complaine.

—◦◦◦—

Beauty is but a Painted Hell.

Fourth Booke of Ayres (1617?).

BEAUTY is but a painted hell :
      Aye me, aye me !
Shee wounds them that admire it,
Shee kils them that desire it.
      Give her pride but fuell,
      No fire is more cruell.

Pittie from ev'ry heart is fled :
      Aye me, aye me !
Since false desire could borrow
Teares of dissembled sorrow,
      Constant vowes turne truthlesse,
      Love cruell, Beauty ruthlesse.

Sorrow can laugh, and Fury sing :
      Aye me, aye me !
My raving griefes discover
I liv'd too true a lover.
      The first step to madnesse
      Is the excesse of sadnesse.

Campion.

Are You, what your Faire Lookes Expresse?

Fourth Booke of Ayres (1617?).

ARE you, what your faire lookes expresse?
  O then be kinde!
From law of nature they digresse
  Whose forme sutes not their minde:
Fairnesse seene in th' outward shape,
Is but th' inward beauties Ape.

Eyes that of earth are mortall made,
  What can they view?
All's but a colour or a shade,
  And neyther alwayes true:
Reason's sight, that is eterne,
Ev'n the substance can discerne.

Soul is the Man: for who will so
  The body name?
And to that power all grace we owe
  That deckes our living frame.
What, or how had housen bin,
But for them that dwell therein?

Love in the bosome is begot,
  Not in the eyes;
No beauty makes the eye more hot,
  Her flames the spright surprise:
Let our loving mindes then meete,
For pure meetings are most sweet.

93

Since She, ev'n Shee.

Fourth Booke of Ayres (1617 ?).

SINCE she, ev'n shee, for whom I liv'd,
　Sweet she by Fate from me is torne,
Why am not I of sence depriv'd,
　Forgetting I was ever borne?
Why should I languish, hating light?
Better to sleepe an endlesse night.

Be't eyther true, or aptly fain'd,
　That some of Lethe's water write,
'Tis their best med'cine that are pain'd
　All thought to loose of past delight.
O would my anguish vanish so!
Happy are they that neyther know.

—◊◊◊—

I Must Complain.

Fourth Booke of Ayres (1617 ?).

I MUST complain, yet doe enjoy my love;
　She is too faire, too rich in lovely parts:
Thence is my grief, for Nature, while she strove
　With all her graces and divinest Arts
To form her too too beautifull of hue,
Shee had no leasure left to make her true.

94

Should I, agriev'd, then wish shee were lesse
    fayre?
  That were repugnant to mine owne desires.
Shee is admir'd, new lovers still repayre,
    That kindles daily love's forgetfull fires.
Rest, jealous thoughts, and thus resolve at
    last,—
Shee hath more beauty than becomes the chast.

—-wWWw-—

Her Fayre In-flaming Eyes.

Fourth Booke of Ayres (1617 ?).

Her fayre inflaming eyes,
  Chiefe authors of my cares,
I prai'd in humblest wise
  With grace to view my teares:
     They beheld me broad awake,
     But, alasse, no ruth would take.

Her lips with kisses rich,
  And words of fayre delight,
I fayrely did beseech,
  To pitty my sad plight:
     But a voyce from them brake forth,
     As a whirlewind from the North.

Then to her hands I fled,
  That can give heart and all;
To them I long did plead,
  And loud for pitty call:
     But, alas, they put mee off,
     With a touch worse then a scoff.

So backe I straight return'd,
  And at her breast I knock'd ;
Where long in vain I mourn'd,
  Her heart so fast was lock'd :
        Not a word could passage finde,
        For a Rocke inclos'd her minde.

Then downe my pray'rs made way
  To those most comely parts,
That make her flye or stay,
  As they affect deserts :
        But her angry feete, thus mov'd,
        Fled with all the parts I lov'd.

Yet fled they not so fast,
  As her enraged minde :
Still did I after haste,
  Still was I left behinde ;
        Till I found 'twas to no end,
        With a Spirit to contend.

—ᴧᴧᴠ—

Turne all Thy Thoughts.

Fourth Booke of Ayres
(1617 ?).

Turne all thy thoughts to eyes,
Turne al thy haires to eares,
Change all thy friends to spies,
And all thy joyes to feares :
        True Love will yet be free,
        In spite of Jealousie.

Campion.

Turne darknesse into day,
Conjectures into truth,
Beleeve what th' envious say,
Let age interpret youth :
    True love will yet be free,
    In spite of Jealousie.

Wrest every word and looke,
Racke ev'ry hidden thought,
Or fish with golden hooke ;
True love cannot be caught.
    For that will still be free,
    In spite of Jealousie.

Your Faire Lookes.

Fourth Booke of Ayres
(1617 ?).

Your faire lookes urge my desire :
　Calme it, sweet, with love !
Stay ; O why will you retire ?
　Can you churlish prove ?
If Love may perswade,
　Love's pleasures, deare, deny not :
Here is a grove secur'd with shade :
　O then be wise, and flye not.

Hark, the Birds delighted sing,
　Yet our pleasure sleepes :
Wealth to none can profit bring,
　Which the miser keepes.
O come, while we may,
　Let's chayne Love with embraces ;
Wee have not all times time to stay,
　Nor safety in all places.

What ill finde you now in this,
　Or who can complaine ?
There is nothing done amisse
　That breedes no man payne.
'Tis now flow'ry May ;
　But ev'n in cold December,
When all these leaves are blowne away,
　This place shall I remember.

And would You Faine the Reason Knowe.

Rosseter's Booke of Ayres. Part II. (1601).

A<small>ND</small> would you faine the reason knowe
Why my sad eies so often flow?
My heart ebs joy, when they doe so,
And loves the moone by whom they go.

And will you aske why pale I looke?
'Tis not with poring on my booke:
My mistris' cheeke my bloud hath tooke,
For her mine owne hath me forsooke.

Do not demaund why I am mute:
Love's silence doth all speech confute.
They set the noat, then tune the Lute;
Herts frame their thoughts, then toongs their
    suit. -

Doe not admire why I admire:
My fever is no other's fire:
Each severall heart hath his desire;
Els proof is false, and truth a lier.

If why I love you should see cause:
Love should have forme like other lawes,
But fancie pleads not by the clawes:
'Tis as the sea, still vext with flawes.

No fault upon my love espie ;
For you perceive not with my eie ;
My pallate to your tast may lie,
Yet please itselfe deliciously.

Then let my sufferance be mine owne ;
Sufficeth it these reasons showne ;
Reason and love are ever knowne
To fight till both be overthrowne.

—\/\/\—

Long have Mine Eies.

Rosseter's Booke of Ayres. Part II. (1601).

Long have mine eies gaz'd with delight,
   Conveying hopes unto my soule ;
In nothing happy, but in sight
   Of her, that doth my sight controule :
But now mine eies must loose their light.

My object now must be the aire ;
   To write in water words of fire ;
And teach sad thoughts how to despaire :
   Desert must quarrel with desire.
All were appeas'd were she not faire.

For all my comfort, this I prove,
   That Venus on the Sea was borne :
If Seas be calme, then doth she love ;
   If stormes arise, I am forlorne ;
My doubtfull hopes, like wind doe move.

If I Hope, I Pine; If I Feare, I Faint and Die.

Rosseter's Booke of Ayres. Part II. (1601).

IF I hope, I pine ; if I feare, I faint and die ;
So betweene hope and fear, I desp'rat lie,
Looking for joy to heaven, whence it should
    come :
But hope is blinde, joy deafe, and I am
    dumbe.

Yet I speake and crie ; but, alas, with words
    of wo :
And joy conceives not them that murmure so.
He that the eares of joy will ever pearse,
Must sing glad noates, or speake in happier
    verse.

—✲✲✲—

Shall Then a Traitorous Kisse.

Rosseter's Booke of Ayres. Part II. (1601). —A. H. B.

SHALL then a traitorous kiss or a smile
All my delights unhappily beguile?
Shall the vow of feigned love receive so rich
    regard,
When true service dies neglected, and wants
    his due reward?

Deeds meritorious soon be forgot,
But one offence no time can ever blot ;
Every day it is renewed, and every night it
    bleeds,
And with bloody streams of sorrow drowns all
    our better deeds.

Beauty is not by desert to be won ;
Fortune hath all that is beneath the sun.
Fortune is the guide of Love, and both of them
    be blind :
All their ways are full of errors, which no true
    feet can find.

No Grave for Woe.

A Booke of Ayres.
Part II. (1601).—A. H. B.

No grave for woe, yet earth my watery tears
    devours ;
Sighs want air, and burnt desires kind pity's
    showers :
Stars hold their fatal course, my joys pre-
    venting :
The earth, the sea, the air, the fire, the heavens
    vow my tormenting.

Yet still I live, and waste my weary days in
    groans,
And with woful tunes adorn despairing moans.

Night still prepares a more displeasing
    morrow;
My day is night, my life my death, and all
    but sense of sorrow.

—ʌⱱⱱ⌐

If I Urge My Kind Desires.

A Booke of Ayres.
Part II. (1601).—A. H. B.

If I urge my kind desires,
She unkind doth them reject;
Women's hearts are painted fires
To deceive them that affect.
I alone love's fires include;
She alone doth them delude.

She hath often vowed her love;
But, alas! no fruit I find.
That her fires are false I prove,
Yet in her no fault I find:
I was thus unhappy born,
And ordained to be her scorn.

Yet if human care or pain,
May the heavenly order change,
She will hate her own disdain,
And repent she was so strange:
For a truer heart than I,
Never lived or loved to die.

Unless there were Consent.

Rosseter's Booke of Ayres. Part II. (1601).
—A. H. B.

Unless there were consent 'twixt hell and
    heaven
  That grace and wickedness should be com-
    bined,
I cannot make thee and thy beauties even :
  Thy face is heaven, and torture in thy mind,
For more than worldly bliss is in thy eye
And hellish torture in thy mind doth lie.

A thousand Cherubins fly in her looks,
  And hearts in legions melt upon their view :
But gorgeous covers wall up filthy books ;
  Be it sin to say that so your eyes do you :
But sure your mind adheres not with your
    eyes,
For what they promise, that your heart denies.

But, O, lest I religion should misuse,
  Inspire me thou, that ought'st thyself to
    know
(Since skilless readers, reading do abuse),
  What inward meaning outward sense doth
    show :
For by thy eyes and heart, chose and con-
    temned,
I waver, whether saved or condemned.

If She Forsake Me.

Rosseter's Booke of Ayres. Part II. (1601). —A. H. B.

IF she forsake me, I must die:
  Shall I tell her so?
Alas, then straight she will reply,
  "No, no, no, no, no!"
If I disclose my desperate state,
She will but make sport thereat,
  And more unrelenting grow.

What heart can long such pains abide?
  Fie upon this love!
I would venture far and wide,
  If it would remove.
But Love will still my steps pursue,
I cannot his ways eschew:
  Thus still helpless hopes I prove.

I do my love in lines commend,
  But, alas, in vain;
The costly gifts that I do send,
  She returns again:
Thus still is my despair procured,
And her malice more assured:
  Then come, Death, and end my pain!

With Spotless Minds.

Song from the " Masque at the Marriage of the Lord Hayes; Twelfth Night, 1606."
"All this time of procession the six cornets, and six chapel voices sung a solemn motet of six parts made upon these words."

WITH spotless minds now mount we to the tree
   Of single chastity.
The root is temperance grounded deep,
Which the cold-juiced earth doth steep :
   Water it desires alone,
   Other drink it thirsts for none :
Therewith the sober branches it doth feed,
   Which though they fruitless be,
Yet comely leaves they breed,
   To beautify the tree.
Cynthia protectress is, and for her sake
We this grave procession make.
Chaste eyes and ears, pure hearts and voices,
Are graces wherein Phœbe most rejoices.

—᭴ᑎᘛᘛᘚ—

Campion.

My Sweetest Lesbia, let us Live and Love.

Rosseter's Booke of Ayres. Part I.

My sweetest Lesbia, let us live and love;
And though the sager sort our deedes reprove,
Let us not way them : heaven's great lampes
    doe dive
Into their west, and strait again revive :
But soone as once set is our little light,
Then must we sleepe one ever-during night.

If all would lead their lives in love like mee,
Then bloudie swords and armour should not
    be ;
No drum nor trumpet peaceful sleepes should
    move,
Unles alar'me came from the campe of love :
But fooles do live, and wast their little light,
And seeke with paine their ever-during night.

When timely death my life and fortune ends,
Let not my hearse be vext with mourning
    friends ;
But let all lovers, rich in triumph, come
And with sweet pastimes grace my happie
    tombe :
And, Lesbia, close up thou my little light,
And crown with love my ever-during night.

Let Him that will be Free.

Rosseter's Booke of Ayres. Part II. (1601).

LET him that will be free and keep his hart
    from care,
Retir'd alone, remaine where no discomforts
    are.
For when the eie doth view his griefe, or hap-
    lesse care his sorrow heares,
Th' impression still in him abides, and ever
    in one shape appeares.

Forget thy griefes betimes; long sorrowe
    breedes long paine,
For joie farre fled from men, will not returne
    againe ;
O happie is the soule which heaven ordained
    to live in endles peace !
His life is a pleasing dreame, and everie houre
    his joyes encrease.

You heavie sprites, that love in sever'd shades
    to dwell,
That nurse despaire and dreame of unrelenting
    hell,
Come sing this happie song, and learne of me
    the Arte of true content !
Loade not your guiltie soules with wrong, and
    heaven then will soone relent.

Campion.

What is a Day.

Rosseter's Booke of Ayres. Part II. (1601). —A. H. B.

WHAT is a day, what is a year
  Of vain delight and pleasure?
Like to a dream it endless dies,
  And from us like a vapour flies :
And this is all the fruit that we find,
  Which glory in worldly treasure.

He that will hope for true delight,
  With virtue must be graced ;
Sweet folly yields a bitter taste,
  Which ever will appear at last :
But if we still in virtue delight,
  Our souls are in heaven placed.

—⁓⌇⁓—

Never Weather-beaten Saile more willing Bent to Shore.

Divine and Morall Songs (1613?).

NEVER weatherbeaten Saile more willing
    bent to shore,
Never tyred Pilgrim's limbs affected slumber
    more,
Then my weary spright now longs to flye out
    of my troubled brest.
O come quickly, sweetest Lord, and take my
    soule to rest !

Ever blooming are the joyes of Heav'n's high
    paradice,
Cold age deafes not there our eares, nor vapour
    dims our eyes:
Glory there the sun outshines; whose beames
    the blessed onely see.
O come quickly, glorious Lord, and raise my
    spright to thee!

—◇◇◇—

Tune Thy Musicke to Thy Hart.
Divine and Morall Songs.

Tune thy Musicke to thy hart,
Sing thy joy with thankes, and so thy sorrow:
    Though Devotion needes not Art,
Sometime of the poore the rich may borrow.

    Strive not yet for curious wayes:
Concord pleaseth more, the lesse 'tis strained;
    Zeale affects not outward prayse,
Onely strives to show a love unfained.

    Love can wondrous things effect,
Sweetest Sacrifice, all wrath appeasing;
    Love the highest doth respect;
Love alone to him is ever pleasing.

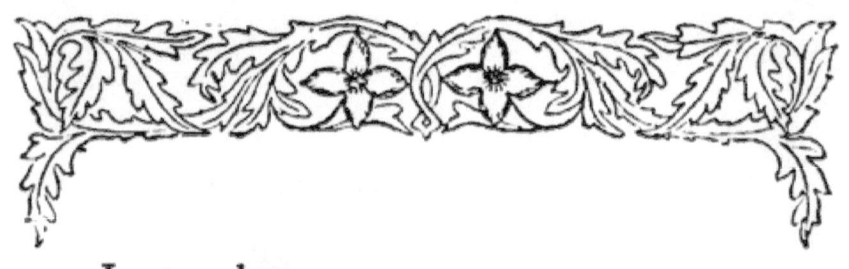

Loe, when Backe Mine Eye.

Divine and Morall Songs (1613 ?).

Loe, when backe mine eye,
   Pilgrim-like, I cast,
What fearefull wayes I spye,
Which, blinded, I securely past !

But now heav'n hath drawne
   From my browes that night ;
As when the day doth dawne,
So cleares my long imprison'd sight.

Straight the caves of hell,
   Drest with flowres I see :
Wherein false pleasures dwell,
That, winning most, most deadly be.

Throngs of masked Feinds,
   Wing'd like Angels, flye :
Ev'n in the gates of Friends
In faire disguise blacke dangers lye.

Straight to Heav'n I rais'd
   My restored sight,
And with loud voyce I prais'd
The Lord of ever-during light.

And since I had stray'd
  From his wayes so wide,
His grace I humbly pray'd
Henceforth to be my guard and guide.

Lift up to Heav'n, sad Wretch, Thy heavy Spright!

Divine and Morall Songs (1613 ?).

LIFT up to heav'n, sad wretch, thy heavy spright!
What though thy sinnes, thy due destruction threat?
The Lord exceedes in mercy as in might;
His ruth is greater, though thy crimes be great.
Repentance needs not feare the heav'n's just rod,
It stays ev'n thunder in the hand of God.

With cheerfull voyce to him then cry for grace!
Thy Faith, and fainting Hope, with Prayer revive;
Remorce for all that truely mourn hath place;
Not God, but men of him themselves deprive:
Strive then, and hee will help; call him, hee'll heare:
The Sonne needes not the Father's fury feare.

As by the Streames of Babilon.

Divine and Morall Songs (1613 ?). A Transcript from Psalm cxxxvii.

As by the streames of Babilon
Farre from our native soyle we sat,
Sweet Sion, thee we thought upon,
And ev'ry thought a teare begat.

Aloft the trees, that spring up there,
Our silent Harps wee pensive hung :
Said they that captiv'd us, Let's heare
Some song which you in Sion sung !

Is then the song of our God fit
To be prophan'd in forraine land ?
O Salem, thee when I forget,
Forget his skill may my right hand !

Fast to the roofe cleave may my tongue,
If mindelesse I of thee be found !
Or if, when all my joyes are sung,
Jerusalem be not the ground !

Remember, Lord, how Edom's race
Cryed in Jerusalem's sad day :
Hurle downe her wals, her towres deface,
And stone by stone all levell lay !

Curst Babel's seede ! for Salem's sake
Just ruine yet for thee remaines !
Blest shall they be thy babes that take
And 'gainst the stones dash out their braines !

Sing a Song of Joy!

Divine and Morall Songs (1613?). A Transcript from the Psalms.

Sing a song of joy!
   Prayse our God with mirth!
His flocke who can destroy?
Is hee not Lord of heav'n and earth?

Sing wee then secure,
   Tuning well our strings!
With voyce, as Eccho pure,
Let us renowne the King of Kings!

First who taught the day
   From the East to rise?
Whom doth the Sunne obey,
When in the Seas his glory dyes?

He the Starres directs
   That in order stand:
Who, heav'n and earth protects,
But hee that fram'd them with his hand?

Angels round attend,
   Wayting on his will;
Arm'd millions hee doth send
To ayde the good, or plague the ill.

Campion.

All that dread his name,
   And his Hests observe,
  His arme will shield from shame :
Their steps from truth shall never swerve.

Let us then rejoyce,
   Sounding loud his prayse :
  So will hee heare our voyce
And blesse on earth our peacefull dayes.

—◊◊◊—

Seeke the Lord, and in his Waies Persever.

Divine and Morall Songs (1613 ?).

Seeke the Lord, and in his waies persever !
   O faint not, but as Eagles flye,
  For his steepe hill is high ;
Then striving gaine the top, and triumph ever !

When with glory there thy browes are crowned,
   New joyes so shall abound in thee,
   Such sights thy soule shall see
That worldly thoughts shall by their beames
   be drowned.

Farewell World, thou masse of meere con-
   fusion !
   False light, with many shadowes dimm'd !
   Old Witch, with new foyles trimm'd !
Thou deadly sleepe of soule, and charm'd
   illusion !

I the King will seeke, of Kings adored,
 Spring of light, tree of grace and bliss,
 Whose fruit so sov'raigne is,
That all who taste it are from death restored.

—⁓⋀⋁⋀⋁⋀⁓—

Lighten, heavy Hart, thy Spright.

Divine and Morall
Songs (1613 ?).

Lighten, heavy hart, thy spright,
 The joyes recall that thence are fled ;
Yeeld thy brest some living light ;
 The man that nothing doth is dead.
Tune thy temper to these sounds,
 And quicken so thy joylesse minde ;
Sloth the worst and best confounds :
 It is the ruine of mankinde.

From her cave rise all distasts,
 Which unresolv'd Despaire pursues ;
Whom, soone after, Violence hasts,
 Herselfe, ungratefull to abuse.
Skies are clear'd with stirring windes,
 Th' unmoved water moorish growes ;
Ev'ry eye much pleasure findes
 To view a streame that brightly flowes.

Most Sweet and Pleasing are Thy Wayes, O God.

Divine and Morall
Songs (1613?).

Most sweet and pleasing are thy wayes, O
  God,
  Like meadowes deckt with Christall streames
    and flowers :
Thy paths no foote prophane hath ever trod,
  Nor hath the proud man rested in thy
    bowers :
There lives no Vultur, no devouring Beare,
But only doves and lambs are harbor'd there.

The Wolfe his young ones to their prey doth
    guide ;
  The foxe his Cubbes with false deceit endues ;
The Lyon's whelpe suckes from his Damme
    his pride ;
  In hers the Serpent malice doth infuse :
The darksome Desart all such beasts contains,
Not one of them in Paradice remaynes.

—ᴧᴧᴧ—

Wise Men.

Divine and Morall Songs (1613?).

Wise men patience never want ;
  Good men pitty cannot hide ;
Feeble spirits onely vant
  Of revenge, the poorest pride :
Hee alone, forgive that can,
Beares the true soule of a man.

Some there are, debate that seeke,
  Making trouble their content,
Happy if they wrong the meeke,
  Vexe them that to peace are bent :
Such undoe the common tye
Of mankinde, societie.

Kindnesse growne is, lately, colde ;
  Conscience hath forgot her part ;
Blessed times were knowne of old,
  Long ere Law became an Art :
Shame deterr'd, not Statutes then,
Honest love was law to men.

Deeds from love, and words, that flow,
  Foster like kinde Aprill showres ;
In the warme Sunne all things grow,
  Wholesome fruits and pleasant flowres :
All so thrives his gentle rayes,
Whereon humane love displayes.

Campion.

View me, Lord, a Worke of Thine.

VIEW me, Lord, a worke of Thine :
Shall I then lye drown'd in night ?
Might Thy grace in mee but shine,
I should seeme made all of light.

But my soul still surfets so
On the poysoned baytes of sinne,
That I strange and ugly growe,
All is darke, and foule within.

Cleanse mee, Lord, that I may kneele
At Thine altar, pure and white :
They that once Thy mercies feele,
Gaze no more on earth's delight.

Worldly joyes, like shadowes, fade
When the heav'nly light appeares ;
But the cov'nants Thou hast made,
Endlesse, know nor dayes nor yeares.

In Thy Word, Lord, is my trust,
To Thy mercies fast I flye ;
Though I am but clay and dust,
Yet Thy grace can lift me high.

De Profundis.   Divine and Morall
                    Songs (1613 ?).

Out of my soule's depth to Thee my cryes
    have sounded :
Let Thine cares my plaints receive, on just feare
    grounded.
Lord, shouldst Thou weigh our faults, who's
    not confounded ?

But with grace Thou censur'st Thine when they
    have erred,
Therefore shall Thy blessed Name be lov'd and
    feared.
Ev'n to Thy throne my thoughts and eyes are
    reared.

Thee alone my hopes attend, on Thee relying ;
In thy sacred word I'le trust, to Thee fast flying,
Long ere the Watch shall breake, the morne
    descrying.

In the mercies of our God who live secured,
May of full redemption rest in Him assured ;
Their sinne-sicke soules by Him shall be recured.

—◇◇◇—

Campion.

Author of Light.

Divine and Morall Songs (1613 ?).

AUTHOR of light, revive my dying sprite!
Redeeme it from the snares of all-confounding
　　night!
　　Lord, light me to Thy blessed way!
For blinde with worldly vaine desires, I wander
　　as a stray.
　　Sunne and Moone, Starres and underlights
　　I see;
But all their glorious beames are mists and
　　darknes, being compar'd to Thee.

Fountaine of health, my soule's deepe wounds
　　recure!
Sweet showres of pitty raine, wash my unclean-
　　nesse pure!
　　One drop of Thy desired grace
The faint and fading heart can raise, and in joy's
　　bosome place.
　　Sinne and Death, Hell and tempting Fiends
　　may rage,
But God his owne will guard, and their sharp
　　paines and griefe in time asswage.

—/ᴧᴧᴧ—

Come, let us Sound.

A Booke of Ayres (1601). Part I.

Come, let us sound with melody the praises
Of the King's King, th' omnipotent Creator,
Author of number, that hath all the world in
            Harmonie framed.

Heav'n is his throne perpetually shining,
His devine power and glorie thence he thunders,
One in all, and all still in one abiding,
            Both Father and Sonne.

O sacred sprite invisible, eternall,
Ev'rywhere, yet unlimited, that all things
Can'st in one moment penetrate, revive me,
            O holy Spirit !

Rescue, O rescue me from earthly darknes,
Banish hence all these elementall objects,
Guide my soule, that thirsts, to the lively Foun-
    taine
            Of thy devinenes !

Cleanse my soule, O God, thy bespotted Image,
Altered with sinne so that heav'nly purenes
Cannot acknowledge me, but in thy mercies,
            O Father of grace !

But when once thy beams do remove my dark-
    ness,
O then I'le shine forth as an Angell of light,
And record, with more than an earthly voice, Thy
            Infinite honours.

Campion.

All Lookes be Pale.

Divine and Morall Songs (1613 ?).

ALL lookes be pale, harts cold as stone,
For Hally now is dead, and gone:
  Hally in whose sight,
   Most sweet sight,
  All the earth late tooke delight.
Ev'ry eye, weepe, with mee!
Joyes drown'd in tears must be.

His Iv'ry skin, his comely hayre,
His Rosie cheekes so cleare, and faire,
  Eyes that once did grace
   His bright face,
  Now in him all want their place.
Eyes and hearts weepe with mee,
For who so kind as hee?

His youth was like an Aprill flowre,
Adorn'd with beauty, love, and powre;
  Glory strow'd his way,
   Whose wreaths gay
  Now are all turn'd to decay.
Then againe, weepe with mee,
None feele more cause then wee.

No more may his wisht sight returne,
His golden Lampe no more can burne;
  Quencht is all his flame;
   His hop't fame
  Now hath left him nought but name.
For him all weepe with mee,
Since more him none shall see.

Time, that Leades.

Song added to the
" Masque at the Lord
Hayes' Marriage, 1606."

TIME, that leades the fatal round,
Hath made his centre in our ground,
   With swelling seas embraced ;
And there at one stay he rests,
And with the Fates keeps holy feasts,
   With pomp and pastime graced.
Light Cupids there do dance and Venus sweetly
     sings
With heavenly notes tuned to sound of silver
     strings :
Their songs are all of joy, no sign of sorrow
     there,
But all as starres glist'ring fair and blithe appear.

—∿∿∿—

What if a Day.

From Richard Alison's
An Hour's Recreation in
Music, 1606.—A. H. B.

WHAT if a day, or a month, or a year
Crown thy delights with a thousand sweet con-
     tentings ?
Cannot a chance of a night or an hour
Cross thy desires with as many sad tormentings ?

Campion.

Fortune, Honour, Beauty, Youth
Are but blossoms dying ;
Wanton Pleasure, doting Love,
Are but shadows flying.
All our joys are but toys,
Idle thoughts deceiving ;
None hath power of an hour
In our lives' bereaving.

Earth's but a point to the world, and a man
Is but a point to the world's compared centre :
Shall then a point of a point be so vain
As to triumph in a silly point's adventure?
All is hazard that we have,
There is nothing biding ;
Days of pleasure are like streams
Through fair meadows gliding.
Weal and woe, time doth go,
Time is never turning :
Secret fates guide our states,
Both in mirth and mourning.

Sweet, Come Again !

A Booke of Ayres (1601). Part II.

Sweet, come again !
  Your happy sight, so much desired,
  Since you from hence are now retired,
I seek in vain :
Still must I mourn
  And pine in longing pain,
  Till you, my life's delight, again
Vouchsafe your wished return.

If true desire,
  Or faithful vow of endless love,
  Thy heart inflamed may kindly move
With equal fire ;
O then my joys,
  So long distraught, shall rest,
  Reposed soft in thy chaste breast,
Exempt from all annoys.

You had the power
  My wand'ring thoughts first to restrain,
  You first did hear my love speak plain !
A child before,
Now it is grown
  Confirmed, do you it keep,
  And let it safe in your bosom sleep,
There ever made your own !

Campion.

And till we meet,
  Teach absence inward art to find,
  Both to disturb and please the mind.
Such thoughts are sweet :
And such remain
  In hearts whose flames are true ;
  Then such will I retain, till you
To me return again.

—∿∿∿—

Reprove not Love

Rosseter.   Part II.
(1601).—A. H. B.

REPROVE not love, though fondly thou hast
      lost
  Greater hopes by loving :
Love calms ambitious spirits, from their breasts
  Danger oft removing :
Let lofty humours mount up on high,
  Down again like to the wind,
While private thoughts, vowed to love,
  More peace and pleasure find.

Love and sweet beauty makes the stubborn
      mild,
  And the coward fearless ;
The wretched miser's care to bounty turns,
  Cheering all things cheerless.
Love chains the earth and heaven,
  Turns the spheres, guides the years in end·
      less peace :
The flowery earth through his power
  Receives her due increase.

The Golden Mean.

Rosseter. Part II. (1601).—A. H. B.

Though far from joy, my sorrows are as far,
And I both between ;
Not too low, nor yet too high
Above my reach, would I be seen.
Happy is he that so is placed,
Not to be envied nor to be disdained or dis-
    graced.

The higher trees, the more storms they endure ;
Shrubs be trodden down :
But the Mean, the Golden Mean,
Doth only all our fortunes crown :
Like to a stream that sweetly slideth
Through the flowery banks, and still in the
    midst his course guideth.

—∿∿∿—

Cruel Laura.

Rosseter. Part II. (1601).

Aye me ! that love should Nature's work
    accuse !
Where cruel Laura still her beauty views,
River, or cloudy jet, or crystal bright,
Are all but servants of herself, delight.

Yet her deformed thoughts, she cannot see ;
And that's the cause she is so stern to me.
Virtue and duty can no favour gain :
A grief, O death ! to live and love in vain.

Had I Foreseen. Rosseter. Part I.
(1601).—A. H. B.

My love hath vowed he will forsake me,
   And I am already sped ;
Far other promise he did make me
   When he had my maidenhead.
If such danger be in playing
   And sport must to earnest turn,
I will go no more a-maying.

Had I foreseen what is ensued,
   And what now with pain I prove,
Unhappy then I had eschewed
   This unkind event of love :
Maids foreknow their own undoing,
   But fear naught till all is done,
When a man alone is wooing.

Dissembling wretch, to gain thy pleasure,
   What didst thou not vow and swear?
So didst thou rob me of the treasure
   Which so long I held so dear.
Now thou provest to me a stranger :
   Such is the vile guise of men
When a woman is in danger.

That heart is nearest to misfortune
   That will trust a feigned tongue ;
When flatt'ring men our loves importune
   They intend us deepest wrong.
If this shame of love's betraying
   But this once I cleanly shun,
I will go no more a-maying.

Though Your Strangenesse.

THOUGH your strangenesse frets my hart,
Yet may not I complaine :
You perswade me, 'tis but Art,
That secret love must faine.
If another you affect,
'Tis but a shew, t'avoid suspect :
Is this faire excusing ?   O no, all is abusing.

Your wisht sight if I desire,
Suspitions you pretend :
Causelesse you yourselfe retire,
While I in vaine attend.
This a Lover whets, you say,
Still made more eager by delay.
Is this faire excusing ?   O no, all is abusing.

When another holds your hand,
You sweare I hold your hart :
When my Rivals close doe stand,
And I sit farre apart,
I am neerer yet then they,
Hid in your bosome, as you say.
Is this faire excusing ?   O no, all is abusing.

Would my Rival then I were,
Some els your secret friend :
So much lesser should I feare,
And not so much attend.

They enjoy you, ev'ry one,
  Yet I must seeme your friend alone.
Is this faire excusing?   O no, all is abusing.

—∿∿∿—

Kinde are Her Answeres.

Third Booke of Ayres (1617?).

Kinde are her answeres,
  But her performance keeps no day ;
  Breaks time, as dancers
  From their own Musicke when they stray :
All her free favors and smooth words,
  Wing my hopes in vaine.
O did ever voice so sweet but only fain ?
  Can true love yeeld such delay,
  Converting joy to pain ?

  Lost is our freedome,
  When we submit to women so :
  Why doe wee neede them
When in their best they worke our woe ?
  There is no wisedome
  Can alter ends by Fate prefixt.
O why is the good of man with evill mixt ?
  Never were dayes yet cal'd two,
  But one night went betwixt.

—∿∿∿—

Dance now and Sing.

" A song and dance of six, two Keepers, two Robin - Hood men, the fantastic Traveller and the Cynic." From the " Masque given by Lord Knowles" (1613). A. H. B.

I.

Dance now and sing; the joy and love we
    owe
Let cheerful voices and glad gestures show :
   The Queen of grace is she whom we receive :
   Honour and state are her guides,
   Her presence they can never leave.
Then in a stately sylvan form salute
   Her ever-flowing grace ;
Fill all the woods with echoed welcomes,
   And strew with flowers this place ;
Let ev'ry bough and plant fresh blossoms
     yield,
   And all the air refine :
Let pleasure strive to please our goddess,
   For she is all divine.

II.

Yet once again let us our measures move,
And with sweet notes record our joyful love.
   An object more divine none ever had :
   Beauty, and heav'n-born worth,
   Mixt in perfection never fade.

Campion.

Then with a dance triumphant let us sing
   Her high advanced praise,
And ev'n to heav'n our gladsome welcomes
   With wings of music raise ;
Welcome, O welcome, ever-honoured Queen,
   To this now-blessed place !
That grove, that bower, that house is happy
   Which you vouchsafe to grace.

—◇◇◇—

Gardener's Song.

A song of a treble and bass, sung by the Gardener's boy and man, to music of instruments, that was ready to second them in the arbour. From the " Masque given by Lord Knowles " (1613).— A. H. B.

I.

WELCOME to this flowery place,
Fair Goddess and sole Queen of grace :
All eyes triumph in your sight,
Which through all this empty space
Casts such glorious beams of light.

II.

Paradise were meeter far
To entertain so bright a star :
But why errs my folly so ?
Paradise is where you are :
Heav'n above, and heav'n below.

III.

Could our powers and wishes meet,
How well would they your graces greet !
Yet accept of our desire :
Roses, of all flowers most sweet,
Spring out of the silly briar.

—⌇⌇⌇—

Gardener's Speech.

From the "Masque given by Lord Knowles" (1613).—A. H. B.

"At the Queen's parting on Wednesday in the afternoon, the Gardener with his man and boy and three handsome country maids, the one bearing a rich bag with linen in it, the second a rich apron, and a third a rich mantle, appear all out of an arbour in the lower garden, and meeting the Queen, the Gardener presents this speech."

Gardener.

STAY, goddess ! stay a little space,
Our poor country love to grace,
Since we dare not too long stay you,
Accept at our hands, we pray you,
These mean presents, to express
Greater love than we profess,
Or can utter now for woe
Of your parting hast'ned so.
Gifts these are, such as were wrought
By their hands that them have brought,

Campion.

Home-bred things, which they presumed,
After I had them perfumed
With my flowery incantation,
To give you in presentation
At your parting.   Come, feat lasses,
With fine curtsies, and smooth faces,
Offer up your simple toys
To the mistress of our joys ;
While we the sad time prolong
With a mournful parting song.

—∿∿∿—

A Song of Three Voices.

From the " Masque given by Lord Knowles" (1613).—A. H. B.

I.

Can you, the author of our joy,
    So soon depart?
Will you revive, and straight destroy?
    New mirth to tears convert?
O that ever cause of gladness
Should so swiftly turn to sadness !

II.

Now as we droop, so will these flowers,
    Barred of your sight :
Nothing avail them heav'nly showers
    Without your heav'nly light.
When the glorious sun forsakes us,
Winter quickly overtakes us.

III.

Yet shall our prayers your ways attend,
　　When you are gone ;
And we the tedious time will spend,
　　Rememb'ring you alone.
Welcome here shall you hear ever,
But the word of parting never.

—⁓⋀⋁⋀⁓—

Advance Your Choral Motions.

A Song from the "Lords' Masque" (1613). —A. H. B.

"According to the humour of this song, the stars moved in an exceeding strange and delightful manner, and I suppose few have ever seen more neat artifice than Master Inigo Jones shewed in contriving their motion, who in all the rest of the workmanship which belonged to the whole invention shewed extraordinary industry and skill, which if it be not as lively exprest in writing as it appeared in view, rob not him of his due, but lay the blame on my want of right apprehending his instructions for the adorning of his art."

I.

ADVANCE your choral motions now,
　　You music-loving lights :
This night concludes the nuptial vow,
　　Make this the best of nights :

Campion.

So bravely crown it with your beams
  That it may live in fame
As long as Rhenus or the Thames
  Are known by either name.

II.

Once more again, yet nearer move
  Your forms at willing view ;
Such fail effects of joy and love
  None can express but you.
Then revel midst your airy bowers
  Till all the clouds do sweat,
That pleasure may be poured in showers
  On this triumphant seat.

III.

Long since hath lovely Flora thrown
  Her flowers and garlands here ;
Rich Ceres all her wealth hath shown,
  Proud of her dainty cheer.
Changed then to human shape, descend,
  Clad in familiar weed,
That every eye may here commend
  The kind delights you breed.

—ᴧᴧᴧᴧ᷍

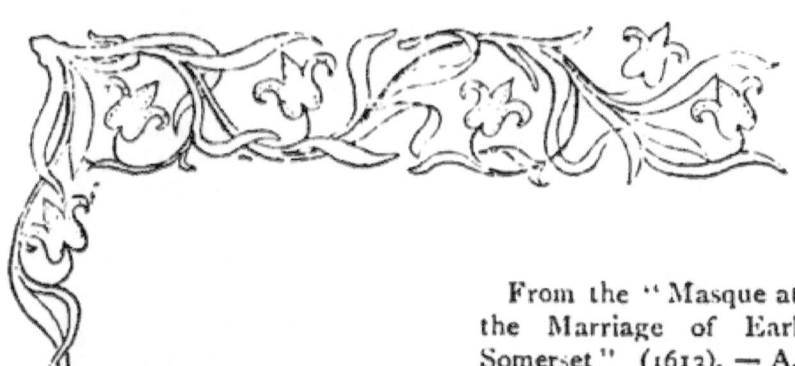

Go, Happy Man.

From the "Masque at the Marriage of Earl Somerset" (1613). — A. H. B. "At the end of this speech, the Queen pulled a branch from the tree and gave it to a nobleman, who delivered it to one of the squires. A song while the Squires descend with the bough toward the scene."

Go, happy man, like th' evening star,
Whose beams to bridegrooms welcome are :
May neither hag, nor fiend withstand
The power of thy victorious hand.
    The uncharmed knights surrender now,
    By virtue of thy raised bough.

Away, enchantments ! vanish quite,
No more delay our longing sight :
'Tis fruitless to contend with Fate,
Who gives us power against your hate.
    Brave knights, in courtly pomp appear,
    For now are you long-looked-for here.

Campion.

Bridal Song.

From the "Lords' Masque" (1613). "The masquers, having every one entertained his lady, begin their first new entering dance : after it, while they breathe, the time is entertained with a dialogue-song." "Disleek" (l. 8), dislike.—A. H. B.

Breathe you now, while Io Hymen
　To the bride we sing :
O how many joys and honours,
　From this match will spring !
Ever firm the league will prove,
Where only goodness causeth love.
Some for profit seek
What their fancies most disleek :
These love for virtue's sake alone :
Beauty and youth unite them both in one.

Chorus.

Live with thy bridegroom happy, sacred bride ;
How blest is he that is for love envied !

The masquers' second dance.

Breathe again, while we with music
　Fill the empty space :
O but do not in your dances
　Yourselves only grace.
Ev'ry one fetch out your fere,
Whom chiefly you will honour here.

Sights most pleasure breed,
When their numbers most exceed.
Choose then, for choice to all is free ;
Taken or left, none discontent must be.

Chorus.

Now in thy revels frolic-fair delight,
To heap joy on this ever-honoured night.

—⋀⋁⋀—

Song.
From the " Lords' Masque "
(1613).—A. H. B.

Orpheus.

ENOUGH of blessing, though too much
Never can be said to such ;
But night doth waste, and Hymen chides,
Kind to bridegrooms and to brides.
Then, singing, the last dance induce,
So let good night present excuse.

The Song.

No longer wrong the night
Of her Hymenæan right ;
A thousand Cupids call away,
Fearing the approaching day ;
The cocks already crow :
　　　Dance then and go !

Campion.

'Tis now Dead Night.

Song addressed "To the most sacred Queen Anne." From the "Songs of Mourning," for Prince Henry, who died at the age of eighteen, Nov. 6th, 1612. He was a friend of poets, and Campion was not the only poet who bewailed his untimely loss.—A. H. B.

I.

'Tis now dead night, and not a light on earth,
　　Or star in heaven, doth shine :
Let now a mother mourn the noblest birth
　　That ever was both mortal and divine.
　　O sweetness peerless ! more than human
　　　　grace !
　　O flowery beauty ! O untimely death !
　　　　Now, Music, fill this place
　　　　With thy most doleful breath :
O singing wail a fate more truly funeral,
Than when with all his sons the sire of Troy
　　did fall.

II.

Sleep, Joy ! die, Mirth ! and not a smile be seen,
　　Or show of heart's content !
For never sorrow nearer touched a Queen,
　　Nor were there ever tears more duly spent.
　　O dear remembrance, full of rueful woe !
　　O ceaseless passion ! O unhuman hour !
　　　　No pleasure now can grow,
　　　　For withered is her flower.
O anguish do thy worst and fury tragical,
Since fate in taking one hath thus disordered all.

Fortune and Glory.

Song addressed "To the most High and Mighty Prince Charles." From the "Songs of Mourning." (1613). — A. H. B.

I.

FORTUNE and Glory may be lost and won,
But when the work of Nature is undone
 That loss flies past returning ;
 No help is left but mourning.
What can to kind youth more despiteful prove
 Than to be robbed of one sole brother ?
 Father and Mother
Ask reverence, a brother only love.
Like age and birth like thoughts and pleasures
 move :
 What gain can he heap up, though showers
 of crowns descend,
 Who for that good must change a brother
 and a friend ?

II.

Follow, O follow yet thy brother's fame,
But not his fate : let's only change the name,
 And find his worth presented
 In thee, by him prevented.
O['e]r past example of the dead be great,
 Out of thyself begin thy story :
 Virtue and glory
Are eminent being placed in princely seat.
Oh, heaven, his age prolong with sacred heat,
 And on his honoured head let all the
 blessings light
 Which to his brother's life men wished, and
 wished them right.

Raving Warre.

A piece of chorus from a Tragedy. From "Observations in the Art of English Poesie" (1602).

"The Dimeter I intend next of all to handle, because it seems to be a part of the Iambick, which is our most naturall and auncient English verse. We may terme this our English march, because the verse answers our warlick forme of march in similitude of number. But call it what you please, for I will not wrangle about names, only intending to set down the nature of it and true structure. It consists of two feete and one odd sillable. The first foote may be made either a Trochy, or a Spondee, or an Iambick at the pleasure of the composer, though most naturally that place affects a Trochy or Spondee; yet by the example of Catullus in his Hendicasillables, I adde in the first place sometimes an Iambick foote. In the second place we must ever insert a Trochy or Tribrack, and so leave the last sillable (as in the end of a verse it is alwaies held) common."

Raving warre begot
In the thirstye sands
Of the Lybian Iles,
Wasts our emptye fields;
What the greedye rage
Of fell wintrye stormes
Could not turne to spoile,
Fierce Bellona now
Hath laid desolate,
Voyd of fruit, or hope.

Lyric Poems.

Th' eger thriftye hinde,
Whose rude toyle reviv'd
Our skie-blasted earth,
Himselfe is but earth,
Left a skorne to fate
Through seditious armes :
And that soile, alive
Which he duly nurst,
Which him duly fed,
Dead his body feeds :
Yet not all the glebe
His tuffe hands manur'd
Now one turfe affords
His poore funerall.
Thus still needy lives,
Thus still needy dyes
Th' unknowne multitude.

Campion.

To the Reader.

Prefixed to Barnabe Barnes' " Four Books of Offices, 1606." In Honour of the Author by Tho: Campion, Doctor in Physic.

Though neither thou dost keep the keys of
  state,
Nor yet the counsels, reader, what of that?
Though th' art no law-pronouncer marked by
  fate,
Nor field-commander, reader, what of that?
Blanch not this book ; for if thou mind'st to be
Virtuous and honest it belongs to thee.
Here is the school of temperance and wit,
Of Justice and all forms that tend to it ;
Here Fortitude doth teach to live and die :
Then, Reader, love this book, or rather buy.

—◁◁◁◁◁—

Neither Buskin now, nor Bays.

L'envoi inscribed to the Reader : from the " Masque at the Marriage of the Lord Hayes."

Neither buskin now, nor bays
Challenge I : a Lady's praise
Shall content my proudest hope.
Their applause was all my scope ;
And to their shrines properly
Revels dedicated be :

8 K   143

Whose soft ears none ought to pierce
But with smooth and gentle verse.
Let the tragic Poem swell,
Raising raging fiends from hell ;
And let epic dactyls range
Swelling seas and countries strange :
Little room small things contains ;
Easy praise quites easy pains.
Suffer them whose brows do sweat
To gain honour by the great :
It's enough if men me name
A retailer of such fame.

Masque at the Marriage of the Lord Hayes.

" Presented before the King's Majesty at White Hall, on twelfth night last (1605), in honour of the Lord Hayes (Sir Jas. Hay), and his bride, daughter and heir to the honourable the Lord Denny, their marriage having been the same day at Court solemnized."

As in battles, so in all other actions that are to be reported, the first, and most necessary part is the description of the place, with his opportunities and properties, whether they be natural or artificial. The great hall (wherein the Masque was presented) received this division, and order. The upper part where the cloth and chair of state were placed, had scaffolds and seats on either side continued to the screen; right before it was made a partition for the dancing-place; on the right hand whereof were consorted ten musicians, with bass and mean lutes, a bandora, a double sackbut, and an harpsichord, with two treble violins; on the other side somewhat nearer the screen were placed nine violins and three lutes, and to answer both the consorts (as it were in a triangle) six cornets, and six chapel voices, were seated almost right against them,

A Masque.

in a place raised higher in respect of the
piercing sound of those instruments; eighteen
foot from the screen, another stage was raised
higher by a yard than that which was prepared
for dancing. This higher stage was all en-
closed with a double veil, so artificially painted,
that it seemed as if dark clouds had hung
before it: within that shroud was concealed
a green valley, with green trees round about
it, and in the midst of them nine golden trees
of fifteen foot high, with arms and branches
very glorious to behold. From the which
grove toward the state was made a broad
descent to the dancing-place, just in the
midst of it; on either hand were two ascents,
like the sides of two hills, drest with shrubs
and trees; that on the right hand leading to
the bower of Flora: the other to the house
of Night; which bower and house were placed
opposite at either end of the screen, and between them both was raised a hill, hanging
like a cliff over the grove below, and on the
top of it a goodly large tree was set, supposed
to be the tree of Diana; behind the which
toward the window was a small descent, with
another spreading hill that climbed up to the
top of the window, with many trees on the
height of it, whereby those that played on the
hautboys at the King's entrance into the hall
were shadowed. The bower of Flora was very
spacious, garnished with all kind of flowers,
and flowery branches with lights in them; the
house of Night ample and stately, with black
pillars, whereon many stars of gold were fixed:

within it, when it was empty, appeared nothing
but clouds and stars, and on the top of it stood
three turrets underpropt with small black
starred pillars, the middlemost being highest
and greatest, the other two of equal proportion : about it were placed on wire artificial
bats and owls, continually moving ; with
many other inventions, the which for brevity
sake I pass by with silence.

Thus much for the place, and now from
thence let us come to the persons.

The Masquers' names were these (whom
both for order and honour I mention in
the first place).

1. Lord WALDEN
2. Sir THOMAS HOWARD.
3. Sir HENRY CAREY, Master of the Jewel
    house.
4. Sir RICHARD PRESTON } Gent. of the K.
5. Sir JOHN ASHLEY   } Privy Chamber.
6. Sir THOMAS JARRET, Pensioner.
7. Sir JOHN DIGBY, one of the King's Carvers.
8. Sir THOMAS BADGER, Master of the
    King's Harriers.
9. Master GORINGE.

Their number nine, the best and amplest of
numbers, for as in music seven notes contain
all variety, the eight[h] being in nature the
same with the first, so in numbering after the
ninth we begin again, the tenth being as it were
the diapason in arithmetic. The number of

A Masque.

nine is framed by the Muses and Worthies, and
it is of all the most apt for change and diversity
of proportion. The chief habit which the
Masquers did use is set forth to your view
in the first leaf: they presented in their feigned
persons the knights of Apollo, who is the father
of heat and youth, and consequently of amorous affections.

The Speakers were in number four.

FLORA,

the queen of flowers, attired in a changeable
taffeta gown, with a large veil embroidered
with flowers, a crown of flowers, and white
buskins painted with flowers.

ZEPHYRUS,

in a white loose robe of sky-coloured taffeta,
with a mantle of white silk, propped with wire,
still waving behind him as he moved; on his
head he wore a wreath of palm deckt with
primroses and violets, the hair of his head
and beard were flaxen, and his buskins white,
and painted with flowers.

NIGHT,

in a close robe of black silk and gold, a black
mantle embroidered with stars, a crown of stars
on her head, her hair black and spangled with
gold, her face black, her buskins black, and
painted with stars; in her hand she bore a
black wand, wreathed with gold.

Campion.

in a close robe of a deep crimson taffeta mingled
with sky-colour, and over that a large loose
robe of a lighter crimson taffeta ; on his head
he wore a wreathed band of gold, with a star
in the front thereof, his hair and beard red, and
buskins yellow.

These are the principal persons that bear
sway in this invention, others that are but
seconders to these, I will describe in their
proper places, discoursing the Masque in order
as it was performed.

As soon as the King was entered the great
Hall, the Hautboys (out of the wood on the
top of the hill) entertained the time till his
Majesty and his train were placed, and then
after a little expectation the consort of ten
began to play an air, at the sound whereof
the veil on the right hand was withdrawn,
and the ascent of the hill with the bower of
Flora were discovered, where Flora and
Zephyrus were busily plucking flowers from
the bower, and throwing them into two
baskets, which two Sylvans held, who were
attired in changeable taffeta, with wreaths
of flowers on their heads. As soon as the
baskets were filled, they came down in this
order ; first Zephyrus and Flora, then the
two Sylvans with baskets after them ; four
Sylvans in green taffeta and wreaths, two
bearing mean lutes, the third, a bass lute,
and the fourth a deep bandora.

As soon as they came to the descent toward
the dancing-place, the consort of ten ceased,

A Masque.

and the four Sylvans played the same air, to
which Zephyrus and the two other Sylvans did
sing these words in a bass, tenor, and treble
voice, and going up and down as they sung
they strewed flowers all about the place.

SONG.

Now hath Flora robbed her bowers
To befriend this place with flowers :
    Strow about, strow about !
The sky rained never kindlier showers.
Flowers with bridals well agree,
Fresh as brides and bridegrooms be :
    Strow about, strow about !
And mix them with fit melody.
Earth hath no princelier flowers
Than roses white and roses red,
But they must still be mingled :
And as a rose new plucked from Venus' thorn,
So doth a bride her bridegroom's bed adorn.

Divers divers flowers affect
For some private dear respect :
    Strow about, strow about !
Let every one his own protect ;
But he's none of Flora's friend
That will not the rose commend.
    Strow about, strow about !
Let princes princely flowers defend :
Roses, the garden's pride,
Are flowers for love and flowers for kings,
In courts desired and weddings :

Campion.

And as a rose in Venus' bosom worn,
So doth a bridegroom his bride's bed adorn.

The music ceaseth and Flora speaks.

FLORA.

Flowers and good wishes Flora doth present,
Sweet flowers, the ceremonious ornament
Of maiden marriage, Beauty figuring,
And blooming youth ; which though we care-
    less fling
About this sacred place, let none profane
Think that these fruits from common hills are
    ta'en,
Or vulgar vallies which do subject lie
To winter's wrath and cold mortality.
But these are hallowed and immortal flowers
With Flora's hands gathered from Flora's
    bowers.
Such are her presents, endless as her love,
And such for ever may this night's joy prove.

ZEPH.

For ever endless may this night's joy prove !
So echoes Zephyrus the friend of Love,
Whose aid Venus implores when she doth bring
Into the naked world the green-leaved spring.
When of the sun's warm beams the nets we
    weave
That can the stubborn'st heart with love deceive.
That Queen of Beauty and Desire by me
Breathes gently forth this bridal prophecy :
Faithful and fruitful shall these bedmates prove,
Blest in their fortunes, honoured in their love.

A Masque.

FLORA.

All grace this night, and, Sylvans, so must you,
Off'ring your marriage song with changes new.

THE SONG IN FORM OF A DIALOGUE.

CAN.

Who is the happier of the two,
      A maid, or wife?

TEN.

Which is more to be desired,
      Peace or strife?

CAN.

What strife can be where two are one,
Or what delight to pine alone?

BAS.

None such true friends, none so sweet life,
As that between the man and wife.

TEN.

A maid is free, a wife is tied.

CAN.

No maid but fain would be a bride.

TEN.

Why live so many single then?
'Tis not I hope for want of men.

Campion.

CAN.

The bow and arrow both may fit,
And yet 'tis hard the mark to hit.

BAS.

He levels fair that by his side
Lays at night his lovely Bride.

CHO.

Sing Io, Hymen ! Io, Io, Hymen !

This song being ended the whole veil is
suddenly drawn, the grove and trees of gold,
and the hill with Diana's tree are at once
discovered.

Night appears in her house with her Nine
Hours, apparelled in large robes of black
taffeta, painted thick with stars, their hairs
long, black, and spangled with gold, on their
heads coronets of stars, and their faces black.
Every Hour bore in his hand a black torch,
painted with stars, and lighted. Night presently descending from her house spake as
followeth.

NIGHT

Vanish, dark veils ! let night in glory shine
As she doth burn in rage : come leave our shrine
You black-haired Hours, and guide us with
    your lights,
Flora hath wakened wide our drowsy sprites :
See where she triumphs, see her flowers are
    thrown,
And all about the seeds of malice sown !

A Masque.

Despiteful Flora, is't not enough of grief
That Cynthia's robbed, but thou must grace
    the thief?
Or didst not hear Night's sovereign Queen
    complain
Hymen had stolen a Nymph out of her train,
And matched her here, plighted henceforth to be
Love's friend, and stranger to virginity?
And makest thou sport for this?

FLORA.

Be mild, stern Night;
Flora doth honour Cynthia, and her right.
Virginity is a voluntary power,
Free from constraint, even like an untouched
    flower
Meet to be gathered when 'tis throughly blown.
The Nymph was Cynthia's while she was her
    own,
But now another claims in her a right,
By fate reserved thereto and wise foresight.

ZEPH.

Can Cynthia one kind virgin's loss bemoan?
How if perhaps she brings her ten for one?
Or can she miss one in so full a train?
Your Goddess doth of too much store complain.
If all her Nymphs would ask advice of me
There should be fewer virgins than there be.
Nature ordained not men to live alone,
Where there are two a woman should be one.

NIGHT.

Thou breath'st sweet poison, wanton Zephyrus,
But Cynthia must not be deluded thus.

Campion.

Her holy forests are by thieves profaned,
Her virgins frighted, and lo, where they stand
That late were Phœbus' knights, turned now
    to trees
By Cynthia's vengement for their injuries
In seeking to seduce her nymphs with love :
Here they are fixt, and never may remove
But by Diana's power that stuck them here.
Apollo's love to them doth yet appear,
In that his beams hath gilt them as they grow,
To make their misery yield the greater show.
But they shall tremble when sad Night doth
    speak,
And at her stormy words their boughs shall
    break.

Toward the end of this speech Hesperus
begins to descend by the house of Night, and
by that time the speech was finished he was
ready to speak.

HESP.

Hail reverend angry Night, hail Queen of
    Flowers,
Mild spirited Zephyrus, hail, Sylvans and Hours.
Hesperus brings peace, cease then your need-
    less jars
Here in this little firmament of stars.
Cynthia is now by Phœbus pacified,
And well content her nymph is made a bride.
Since the fair match was by that Phœbus graced
Which in this happy Western Isle is placed
As he in heaven, one lamp enlight'ning all
That under his benign aspect doth fall.

157

A Masque.

Deep oracles he speaks, and he alone
For arts and wisdom's meet for Phœbus' throne.
The Nymph is honoured, and Diana pleased:
Night, be you then, and your black Hours
    appeased:
And friendly listen what your queen by me
Farther commands: let this my credence be,
View it, and know it for the highest gem,
That hung on her imperial diadem.

NIGHT.

I know, and honour it, lovely Hesperus,
Speak then your message, both are welcome to
    us.

HESP.

Your Sovereign from the virtuous gem she sends
Bids you take power to retransform the friends
Of Phœbus, metamorphosed here to trees,
And give them straight the shapes which they
    did lese.
  This is her pleasure.

NIGHT.

Hesperus, I obey,
Night must needs yield when Phœbus gets the
    day.

FLORA.

Honoured be Cynthia for this generous deed.

ZEPH.

Pity grows only from celestial seed.

Campion.

NIGHT.

If all seem glad, why should we only lower?
Since t'express gladness we have now most
    power.
Frolic, graced captives, we present you here
This glass, wherein your liberties appear:
Cynthia is pacified, and now blithe Night
Begins to shake off melancholy quite.

ZEPH.

Who should grace mirth and revels but the
    Night?
Next Love she should be goddess of delight.

NIGHT.

'Tis now a time when (Zephyrus) all with danc-
    ing
Honour me, above Day my state advancing.
I'll now be frolic, all is full of heart,
And ev'n these trees for joy shall bear a part:
Zephyrus, they shall dance.

ZEPH.

Dance, Goddess? how?

NIGHT.

Seems that so full of strangeness to you now?
Did not the Thracian harp long since the same?
And (if we rip the old records of fame)
Did not Amphion's lyre the deaf stones call,
When they came dancing to the Theban wall?
Can music then joy? joy mountains moves
And why not trees? joy's powerful when it loves.
Could the religious Oak speak Oracle

A Masque.

Like to the Gods? and the tree wounded tell
T'Æneas his sad story? have trees therefore
The instruments of speech and hearing more
Than th' have of pacing, and to whom but
    Night
Belong enchantments? who can more affright
The eye with magic wonders?   Night alone
Is fit for miracles, and this shall be one
Apt for this Nuptial dancing jollity.
Earth, then be soft and passable to free
These fettered roots : joy, trees! the time draws
    near
When in your better forms you shall appear.
Dancing and music must prepare the way,
There's little tedious time in such delay.

   This spoken, the four Sylvans played on
their instruments the first strain of this song
following : and at the repetition thereof the
voices fell in with the instruments which were
thus divided : a treble and a bass were placed
near his Majesty, and another treble and bass
near the grove, that the words of the song
might be heard of all, because the trees of gold
instantly at the first sound of their voices began
to move and dance according to the measure
of the time which the musicians kept in singing,
and the nature of the words which they delivered.

SONG.

    Move now with measured sound,
    You charmed grove of gold,
    Trace forth the sacred ground
    That shall your forms unfold.

Campion.

Diana and the starry Night for your Apollo's
    sake
Endue your Sylvan shapes with power this
    strange delight to make.
Much joy must needs the place betide where
    trees for gladness move :
A fairer sight was ne'er beheld, or more ex-
    pressing love.

        Yet nearer Phœbus' throne
        Meet on your winding ways,
        Your bridal mirth make known
        In your high-graced Hayes.

Let Hymen lead your sliding rounds, and guide
    them with his light,
While we do Io Hymen sing in honour of this
    night,
Join three by three, for so the night by triple
    spell decrees,
Now to release Apollo's knights from these en-
    chanted trees.

    This dancing-song being ended, the golden
trees stood in ranks three by three, and Night
ascended up to the grove, and spake thus,
touching the first three severally with her
wand.

NIGHT.

By virtue of this wand, and touch divine,
These Sylvan shadows back to earth resign :
Your native forms resume, with habit fair,
While solemn music shall enchant the air.

A Masque.

Presently the Sylvans with their four instruments, and five voices, began to play, and sing together the song following ; at the beginning whereof that part of the stage whereon the first three trees stood began to yield, and the three foremost trees gently to sink, and this was effected by an engine placed under the stage. When the trees had sunk a yard they cleft in three parts, and the Masquers appeared out of the tops of them, the trees were suddenly conveyed away, and the first three Masquers were raised again by the engine. They appeared then in a false habit, yet very fair, and in form not much unlike their principal and true robe. It was made of green taffeta cut into leaves, and laid upon cloth of silver, and their hats were suitable to the same.

SONG OF TRANSFORMATION.

Night and Diana charge,
  And th' Earth obeys,
Opening large
  Her secret ways,
While Apollo's charmed men
  Their forms receive again.
Give gracious Phœbus honour then,
And so fall down, and rest behind the train,
Give gracious Phœbus honour then,
And so fall, &c.

When those words were sung, the three Masquers made an honour to the King, and so falling back, the other six trees, three by

three, came forward, and when they were
in their appointed places, Night spake again
thus :

NIGHT.

Thus can celestials work in human fate,
Transform and form as they do love or hate ;
Like touch and change receive. The Gods
    agree :
The best of numbers is contained in three.

THE SONG OF TRANSFORMATION AGAIN.

Night and Diana, &c.

Then Night touched the second three trees
and the stage sunk with them as before : and
in brief the second three did in all points as
the first. Then Night spake again.

NIGHT.

The last, and third of nine, touch, magic
    wand,
And give them back their forms at Night's
    command.

Night touched the third three trees, and the
same charm of Night and Diana was sung
the third time ; the last three trees were trans-
formed, and the Masquers raised, when
presently the first Music began his full
Chorus.

Again this song revive and sound it high :
Long live Apollo, Britain's glorious eye !

A Masque.

This chorus was in manner of an Echo, seconded by the cornets, then by the consort of ten, then by the consort of twelve, and by a double chorus of voices standing on either side, the one against the other, bearing five voices apiece, and sometime every chorus was heard severally, sometime mixed, but in the end altogether: which kind of harmony so distinguished by the place, and by the several nature of instruments, and changeable conveyance of the song, and performed by so many excellent masters as were actors in that music (their number in all amounting to forty-two voices and instruments), could not but yield great satisfaction to the hearers.

While this chorus was repeated twice over, the nine masters in their green habits solemnly descended to the dancing-place, in such order as they were to begin their dance, and as soon as the chorus ended, the violins, or consort of twelve began to play the second new dance, which was taken in form of an echo by the cornets, and then catched in like manner by the consort of ten (sometime they mingled two musics together; sometime played all at once); which kind of echoing music rarely became their sylvan attire, and was so truly mixed together, that no dance could ever be better graced than that, as (in such distraction of music) it was performed by the masquers. After this dance Night descended from the grove, and addressed her speech to the masquers, as followeth.

Campion.

Phœbus is pleased, and all rejoice to see
His servants from their golden prison free.
But yet since Cynthia hath so friendly smiled,
And to you tree-born knights is reconciled,
First ere you any more work undertake,
About her tree solemn procession make,
Diana's tree, the tree of Chastity,
That placed alone on yonder hill you see.
These green-leaved robes, wherein disguised
    you made
Stealths to her nymphs through the thick
    forest's shade,
There to the goddess offer thankfully,
That she may not in vain appeased be.
The Night shall guide you, and her Hours
    attend you
That no ill eyes, or spirits shall offend you.

At the end of this speech Night began to
lead the way alone, and after her an Hour
with his torch, and after the Hour a masquer ;
and so in order one by one, a torch-bearer and
a masquer, they march on towards Diana's
tree. When the masquers came by the house
of Night, every one by his Hour received his
helmet, and had his false robe plucked off,
and, bearing it in his hand, with a low honour
offered it at the tree of Chastity, and so in his
glorious habit, with his Hour before him,
marched to the bower of Flora. The shape
of their habit the picture before discovers, the
stuff was of carnation satin laid thick with
broad silver lace, their helmets being made

of the same stuff. So through the bower of
Flora they came, where they joined two torch-
bearers, and two masquers, and when they
past down to the grove, the Hours parted on
either side, and made way between them for
the masquers, who descended to the dancing-
place in such order as they were to begin their
third new dance. All this time of procession
the six cornets, and six chapel voices sung
a solemn motet of six parts made upon these
words.

With spotless minds now mount we to the tree
        Of single chastity.
The root is temperance grounded deep,
Which the cold-juiced earth doth steep:
        Water it desires alone,
        Other drink it thirsts for none:
Therewith the sober branches it doth feed,
        Which though they fruitless be,
Yet comely leaves they breed,
        To beautify the tree.
Cynthia protectress is, and for her sake
We this grave procession make.
Chaste eyes and ears, pure hearts and voices,
Are graces wherein Phœbe most rejoices.

    The motet being ended, the violins began the
third new dance, which was lively performed by
the masquers, after which they took forth the
ladies, and danced the measures with them;
which being finished, the masquers brought
the ladies back again to their places: and
Hesperus with the rest descended from the

grove into the dancing-place, and spake to the
masquers as followeth.

HESPERUS.

Knights of Apollo, proud of your new birth,
Pursue your triumphs still with joy and mirth :
Your changed fortunes, and redeemed estate,
Hesperus to your Sovereign will relate.
'Tis now high time he were far hence retired,
Th' old bridal friend, that ushers Night desired
Through the dim evening shades, then taking
    flight
Gives place and honour to the nuptial Night.
I, that wished evening star, must now make
    way
To Hymen's rights much wronged by my delay.
But on Night's princely state you ought t'
    attend,
And t' honour your new reconciled friend.

NIGHT.

Hesperus as you with concord came, ev'n so
'Tis meet that you with concord hence should
    go.
Then join you, that in voice and art excel,
To give this star a musical farewell.

A DIALOGUE OF FOUR VOICES, TWO BASSES
AND TWO TREBLES.

1. Of all the stars which is the kindest
        To a loving Bride ?
2. Hesperus when in the west
        He doth the day from night divide.

A Masque.

1. What message can be more respected
   Than that which tells wished joys shall be
       effected?
2. Do not Brides watch the evening star?
1. O they can discern it far.
2. Love Bridegrooms revels?
                        1. But for fashion.
2. And why? 1. They hinder wished occasion.
2. Longing hearts and new delights,
   Love short days and long nights.

CHORUS.

Hesperus, since you all stars excel
In bridal kindness, kindly farewell, farewell.

While these words of the Chorus (*kindly
farewell, farewell*) were in singing often
repeated, Hesperus took his leave severally
of Night, Flora, and Zephyrus, the Hours
and Sylvans, and so while the chorus was
sung over the second time, he was got up to
the grove, where turning again to the singers,
and they to him, Hesperus took a second
farewell of them, and so past away by the
house of Night. Then Night spake these
two lines, and therewith all retired to the
grove where they stood before.

NIGHT.

Come, Flora, let us now withdraw our train
That th' eclipsed revels may shine forth again.

Now the masquers began their lighter dances
as corantoes, levaltas and galliards, wherein
when they had spent as much time as they

Campion.

thought fit, Night spake thus from the grove, and in her speech descended a little into the dancing-place.

NIGHT.

Here stay: Night leaden-eyed and sprited
   grows,
And her late Hours begin to hang their brows.
Hymen long since the bridal bed hath drest,
And longs to bring the turtles to their nest.
Then with one quick dance sound up your
   delight,
And with one song we'll bid you all good-night.

At the end of these words, the violins began the 4 new dance, which was excellently discharged by the Masquers, and it ended with a light change of music and measure. After the dance followed this dialogue of 2 voices, a bass and tenor sung by a Sylvan and an Hour.

TEN. SYLVAN.

Tell me, gentle Hour of Night,
Wherein dost thou most delight?

BAS. HO.

Not in sleep.

SYL.

   Wherein then?

HOUR.

In the frolic view of men?

SYL.

Lovest thou music?

A Masque.

HOUR.

O 'tis sweet.

SYL.

What's dancing?

HOUR.

Ev'n the mirth of feet.

SYL.

Joy you in fairies and in elves?

HOUR.

We are of that sort ourselves.
But, Sylvan, say why do you love
Only to frequent the grove?

SYL.

Life is fullest of content,
Where delight is innocent.

HOUR.

Pleasure must vary, not be long.
Come then let's close, and end our song.

CHORUS.

Yet, ere we vanish from this princely sight,
Let us bid Phœbus and his states good-
night.

This chorus was performed with several
Echoes of music, and voices, in manner as
the great chorus before. At the end whereof
the Masquers, putting off their vizards and

Campion.

helmets, made a low honour to the King, and
attended his Majesty to the banqueting place.

TO THE READER.

Neither buskin now, nor bays
Challenge I : a Lady's praise
Shall content my proudest hope.
Their applause was all my scope ;
And to their shrines properly
Revels dedicated be :
Whose soft ears none ought to pierce
But with smooth and gentle verse.
Let the tragic Poem swell,
Raising raging fiends from hell ;
And let epic dactyls range
Swelling seas and countries strange :
Little room small things contains ;
Easy praise quites easy pains.
Suffer them whose brows do sweat
To gain honour by the great :
It's enough if men me name
A retailer of such fame.

—◇◇◇—

Shows and Nightly Revels.

Additional song, from the "Lord Hayes' Masque." "Though the airs were devised only for dancing, yet they are here set forth with words that they may be sung to the lute or viol." (See also song on p. 124.)

Shows and nightly revels, signs of joy and
    peace,
Fill royal Britain's Court, while cruel war far
    off doth rage, for ever hence exiled.
Fair and princely branches with strong arms
    increase
From that deep-rooted tree whose sacred
    strength and glory foreign malice hath
    beguiled.
Our divided kingdoms now in friendly kindred
    meet
And old debate to love and kindness turns, our
    power with double force uniting ;
Truly reconciled, grief appears at last more
    sweet
Both to ourselves .and faithful friends, our
    undermining foes affrighting.

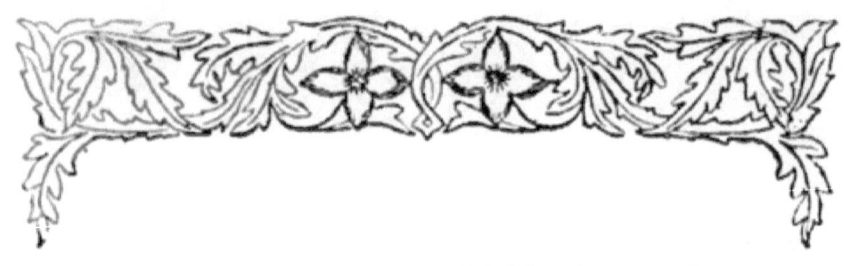

Triumph Now.

Additional song, from the " Lord Hayes' Masque " (1606).

A. H. B.

Triumph now with joy and mirth !
   The God of Peace hath blessed our land :
We enjoy the fruits of earth
   Through favour of His bounteous hand.

We through His most loving grace
   A king and kingly seed behold,
Like a sun with lesser stars
   Or careful shepherd to his fold :
Triumph then, and yield Him praise
That gives us blest and joyful days.

FINIS.

173